"So by your ground rules, what would you call this no-strings verbal contract you're proposing, Dixon? A nonengagement? A disengagement? An unengagement?" She nodded thoughtfully. "Yes, an unengagement. I like the sound of that. I, Alexandra, take you, Dixon, to be my unlawfully unwedded unhusband." She slid her arms around his neck.

Dixon grabbed her forearms. "Which brings us to my second condition."

Pressing her body to his, Alexandra nipped at his lower lip. "Have your lawyer talk to my lawyer, Yano."

"But you don't understand—"

She dragged his face down to meet hers and kissed him until his head swam.

"The ground rules," he protested, albeit feebly.

"Forget the ground rules. There's only one rule in an unengagement: There are no rules. Okay?"

"But—" He opened his mouth to argue the point and Alexandra immediately took advantage. Her soft lips and clever, darting tongue proved devastating to his train of thought.

"Oh, hell," he said with a groan.

When they broke apart, both of them gasping for air, Dixon lifted her into his arms and carried her to the living room. He settled on the sofa with Alexandra on his lap.

"Just like a romance hero."

WHAT ARE *LOVESWEPT* ROMANCES?

They are stories of true romance and touching emotion. We believe those two very important ingredients are constants in our highly sensual and very believable stories in the LOVE-SWEPT line. Our goal is to give you, the reader, stories of consistently high quality that may sometimes make you laugh, sometimes make you cry, but are always fresh and creative and contain many delightful surprises within their pages.

Most romance fans read an enormous number of books. Those they truly love, they keep. Others may be traded with friends and soon forgotten. We hope that each LOVESWEPT romance will be a treasure—a "keeper." We will always try to publish

LOVE STORIES YOU'LL NEVER FORGET
BY AUTHORS YOU'LL ALWAYS REMEMBER

The Editors

Loveswept ® 865

UPON A MIDNIGHT CLEAR

CATHERINE MULVANY

BANTAM BOOKS
NEW YORK · TORONTO · LONDON · SYDNEY · AUCKLAND

UPON A MIDNIGHT CLEAR

A Bantam Book / December 1997

ISBN 0-553-44605-3

Published simultaneously in the United States and Canada

Bantam Books are published by Bantam Books, a division of Bantam Dou-
bleday Dell Publishing Group, Inc. Its trademark, consisting of the words
"Bantam Books" and the portrayal of a rooster, is Registered in U.S. Patent
and Trademark Office and in other countries. Marca Registrada. Bantam
Books, 1540 Broadway, New York, New York 10036.

PRINTED IN THE UNITED STATES OF AMERICA

OPM   10 9 8 7 6 5 4 3 2 1

For Jim Cooley
In Loving Memory
IYQ2, Daddy.

ONE

The dead woman walked into Dixon Yano's office a little after three on Wednesday afternoon. She wore dark glasses and a wig, but Dixon recognized her right away from her obituary photograph in the *Gazette:* Alexandra Roundtree, daughter of mystery novelist Regina Roundtree.

"You don't look Japanese," she said by way of greeting.

"You don't look dead."

"Touché." She smiled, disclosing perfect white teeth.

Glancing down at the newspaper on his desk, then back up at the woman, he realized the grainy picture didn't do her justice. With classic features and flawless skin, Alexandra Roundtree was a "10." Maybe even an "11."

Dixon jumped to his feet, suddenly conscious of the fact that he needed a haircut. A shave wouldn't have come amiss, either. He rubbed absently at his stubbly jaw. His mother kept telling him he needed to dress more professionally. She'd bought him a tie every Christmas for the last five years. Not that a tie would have looked anything short of ludicrous with the sweat-shirt and jeans he was wearing now. "Have a seat."

His prospective client settled gracefully on the ugly gray chair across the desk from him and removed her sunglasses.

Dixon sat, schooling his features to remain impassive, no easy task since her eyes, though distinctly unusual—the left one a clear hazel, the right a bright blue—were as startlingly beautiful as the rest of her. If only she would take off that ugly black wig. According to the picture, her own hair was a blonde-streaked brown that fell past her shoulders in thick waves. Cindy Crawford hair, the kind that practically invited a man to run his fingers through it.

Oblivious to his reactions, the young woman reached out, picked up the newspaper, and studied it a minute in silence. " 'Local Writer Loses Daughter,' " she read, " 'Alexandra Roundtree, twenty-seven-year-old daughter of best-selling mystery novelist Regina Roundtree, died at home, December seventeenth, of natural causes. Services pending.' " She made a face. "Pathetic, isn't it? I can't even get top billing in the headline of my own obituary."

Dixon noted the self-deprecating smile and the hint of some darker emotion shadowing her eyes. Unusual eyes, unusual woman, unusual situation. "What can I do for you, Ms. Roundtree?"

"You're a private detective, right?"

"Private investigator," he corrected automatically.

"Private investigator. Sorry." She rummaged in her purse and drew out a wad of money. "I want to hire you,

Mr. Yano. Here's a thousand dollars as a retainer." She tossed a stack of hundreds on the desk between them. "Help me find my killer."

Just his luck. The first paying customer all week and she was looney tunes. "What killer? You're not dead."

She frowned. "Not yet, but it'll be a miracle if I make it to Christmas. Someone is trying to murder me."

"The obituary said 'natural causes.' "

She gave him a look. "The obituary's a fake, the theory being that if the person threatening me thought I was dead, it might buy me a little time."

"Good strategy. How'd you get the *Gazette* to play along?"

"My uncle's the publisher." She fell silent, staring in apparent fascination at the black leather purse she clenched in her hands. The muffled noise of holiday traffic on the street below sounded loud in the silence.

Dixon watched her closely. Body language betrayed even the best liars.

Alexandra Roundtree squared her jaw and lifted her gaze to meet his. "Over the past couple of weeks, Mr. Yano, I've started having accidents. Only I'm not convinced they *are* accidents."

Dixon relaxed. Confusion, yes. Fear, definitely. But above all, what he read in her face was integrity. "Tell me about it." He paused with his finger above the record button on his tape recorder. "You don't mind if I tape this, do you?"

"Go ahead." She frowned as if she were trying to organize her thoughts. "The first hint of trouble was the exploding reindeer."

Alert for potential clients, Dixon always read the local paper thoroughly and he sure as hell would have noticed any mention of an exploding reindeer. Must have heard her wrong. He shoved his hair behind his ears. "I'm sorry. I thought you said 'exploding reindeer.'"

"I did say 'exploding reindeer.' Eight of them. Nine if you count Rudolph."

"Rudolph." Dixon leaned back in his chair, stretching his legs out in front of him and crossing his arms over his chest. Okay, so she was telling the truth, or at least what she believed to be the truth. Damn. Not a liar, just delusional.

"They were part of a window display at Gemini Gifts. That's the shop my sister and I own. The reindeer were trimmed with strings of Christmas lights that all went off like fireworks. Poor Rudolph's nose exploded into a million fragments of red glass. The jolt knocked me flat and blew every light on our block. At the time I wasn't suspicious. We found a couple of frayed wires, so I dismissed the whole thing as an accident."

"Quite honestly, it does sound like an accident."

"Wait. There's more. The very next day, Saturday before last, I came within millimeters of being squashed by a giant gingerbread house."

Dixon tried hard to keep his expression void of skepticism.

"Part of a float in the Christmas parade," she continued. "My sister, Amanda, and I were on the committee responsible for getting everybody lined up in the right order. Just as the parade was about to begin the whole float suddenly collapsed. If Mandy hadn't pulled me out of harm's way, I'd have been buried under an eight-foot slab of fake gingerbread, nine bazillion gumdrops, and sixteen Girl Scouts dressed as elves."

Dixon blinked. Not to mention two turtledoves and a

partridge in a pear tree. "Right." He cleared his throat. "Again, it could have been—probably was—an accident."

"And I suppose it was just an accident when Santa Claus stole my purse and shoved me down the escalator at the mall?" Alexandra Roundtree tilted her chin at a pugnacious angle.

God, she was a looker. Too damn bad she was so paranoid. "A mugger?" he suggested.

"That's what the police said."

"You don't sound convinced."

"I never carry much money in my purse—"

He raised an eyebrow and flicked the pile of cash with his forefinger.

"All right, hardly ever. The point is I'm not a prime target for a pickpocket, yet of all the people in the mall, that thieving Saint Nick chose to victimize me."

"A crime was committed all right, but I'm with the police here." Dixon shrugged. "I see no evidence of attempted murder."

"What would you consider evidence of attempted murder? A bullet hole between my eyes? A knife in my back?" Tight-lipped, she dug through the contents of her bag once again. "How about this? It came in the mail yesterday." She shoved a sheet of cheap, lined notebook paper into his hands. Someone had pasted together letters cut from the newspaper to form a crude message.

" 'Beware the mistletoe or Christmas may be hazardous to your health,' " he read aloud, and nodded. "Okay, I suppose that could be construed as a threat, but I still don't feel there's a case here. Sorry, Ms. Roundtree." He scooped up the money and held it out to her.

Benjamin Franklin seemed to stare at him accusingly.

Christmas was just around the corner, and an extra thousand dollars was nothing to turn his nose up at.

Ignoring the money, Alexandra stood, then paced restlessly for a few seconds before pausing at the window.

He watched, fascinated, as she chewed at her full lower lip. He wouldn't mind nibbling at that lip himself. She was standing directly under the mistletoe, practically begging to be kissed. The situation was tempting. The woman was tempting. If only . . .

She stared down at the ice-covered street, though he was pretty sure it wasn't the inadequacy of the city maintenance crew that was wrinkling her brow. When she finally spoke, her voice was pitched so low that he had trouble hearing her. "This was a stupid idea. The danger's all in my head anyway, according to Mark."

"Mark?"

"Mark Jordan, my fiancé."

"Ah." Dixon felt as if she'd punched him in the gut. She glanced toward him. "You know Mark?"

"Only by sight." Two years before, Colleen Jordan, the then Mrs. Mark Jordan, had hired Dixon to follow her cheating husband. In the one week Dixon had shadowed the man, Jordan managed to have assignations with six different women in four different motels, which Dixon figured was some kind of record, at least for a small town like Brunswick. Delusional or not, Alexandra Roundtree deserved better than a jerkwad like Mark Jordan.

She turned, so she stood in profile to him. A wistful smile tilted the corner of her mouth. "It was a whirlwind courtship. We met last year at a ski lodge in Sun Valley, got engaged a week later. Mark was so charming, so supportive, though lately . . ."

She straightened and swiveled to face him again, as if suddenly realizing she'd strayed off the subject. "Nobody takes the threat seriously—nobody except my mother. She's the one who suggested I contact you."

"Yes, I've met your mother," Dixon said dryly. Talk about your certifiable nutcases. Regina Roundtree, a woman with a penchant for eccentric hats, was well-known in Brunswick and beyond. Rumor had it she'd once attended a garden party at the White House in a floppy-brimmed confection of aluminum cans crocheted together with fishing line.

From his chair behind the desk, all Dixon could see out the second-story window of Yano Investigations was a slice of bright blue eastern Oregon sky and the damaged top floor of the historic Stockton Building directly across the street. The view was nothing to brag about, but it did provide a nice backdrop for Alexandra, its angles contrasting nicely with her curves.

"Much as I'd like to take your money, Ms. Roundtree, I have to say—"

Suddenly the window shattered, spraying shards of glass.

Alexandra Roundtree fell to the floor.

He thought for one horrible moment that the bullet had found its target, then realized he was the one who was bleeding. Luckily, the deadly projectile had only creased the skin of his upper arm before burying itself in the far wall.

Dixon dropped to all fours, carefully picking his way through broken glass to crawl to Alexandra's side. "Are you all right?"

She nodded, white-faced. A few small cuts marred the

perfection of her face, but none looked serious enough to require immediate medical attention.

"Now do you believe me?" Her voice shook, but he could tell she was more angry than frightened.

He moved toward his desk in a crouched position. She started to get up to follow.

"Stay down." The order came out more sharply than he'd intended.

She flinched, then frowned. "Why? You're not."

Dixon grabbed his .38 from the top drawer. "I'm not a target."

Her gaze followed his every move. "What are you doing? You're not going to leave me here alone, are you?"

He tossed her the cell phone. "Call the police."

"Why can't you do it?"

"That shot came from across the street. I'm going to try to cut the shooter off before he has time to make a getaway. Call the cops. Tell them what happened."

Without waiting to see if she followed his instructions, Dixon ran down the back stairs, then cut through the pet store below. Charging out the front door to the street, where traffic clogged both lanes, Dixon dodged quickly through the cars, careful to avoid the icy patches left over from the big snowstorm they'd had Thanksgiving weekend.

A fire two years earlier had gutted one wing of the Stockton Building and severely damaged the top floor of the main section. The wing had succumbed to the wrecker's ball shortly after the flames were doused, but the owners were gradually refurbishing the main building with an eye to leasing it out as office space.

Dixon entered through the main doors into a huge

room, dominated by a massive stone fireplace. The room had been the lobby back in the days when the Stockton was a hotel. Now it seemed to be temporary headquarters for the contractors hired to do the remodeling. Two men in flannel shirts and baggy jeans were hauling a load of drywall up the curved staircase.

"Anyone come down the stairs in the last couple minutes?"

"Nope." The man who answered had a Fu Manchu mustache and a wad of tobacco tucked under his lip.

"How about the elevator?"

"Broke down." The man spat in a baby-food jar he evidently carried for just that purpose.

"Any other way out of the building?"

"Fire escape. Why? What's the problem?"

"Somebody just loosed a round through my office window across the way. I figure the shot had to come from this building." Dixon headed out to check the fire escape.

The construction worker shouted after him. "We see anybody looks suspicious, we'll drop a load of Sheetrock on him, okay?" He grinned, revealing crooked, nicotine-stained teeth.

Dixon gave him a thumbs-up and hurried around to the alley. The fire escape was empty. Either the gunman had already made his getaway or he was hiding somewhere inside.

Cursing creatively, Dixon jogged back around front just in time to see two city police cars pulling to the curb. He recognized the driver of the first, Officer Cesar Rios. They'd been rookies together way back when. Cesar had been with the city ever since. Dixon, on the other hand, had decided shortly after his first free-for-all drug bust that he'd rather chase deadbeat dads and cheating spouses for a living than set himself up as a target for crazies with guns—which seemed pretty ironic at the moment, what with blood soaking the sleeve of his gray sweatshirt.

"What's the story, Dix?" With a bulletproof vest under his uniform and a bulky winter coat on top, Cesar looked even more intimidating than usual. "Is that blood?"

"Yeah, mine." Dixon explained the situation. "I figure either the guy got away before I made it over here or he's still hiding somewhere in the building."

"We'll check it out." Cesar waved to his partner. "Andy, you go around and keep an eye on the fire escape. I'll do a room-by-room search." He turned back to Dixon. "You wait here. I might have more questions for you later." He started for the entrance at a jog, yelling over his shoulder, "And for Pete's sake, put your gun away. The citizens tend to freak when they see men who look like wild-eyed psychos dripping blood and brandishing firearms."

"Dripping blood?" Dixon eased the pistol into his waistband and tugged the sweatshirt over it. "Hell, I stopped dripping five minutes ago." Cesar didn't respond; he was already inside.

Dixon stared intently at the entrance. He was ninety percent sure the shooter was long gone. Nonetheless, he focused his full attention on the double doors. Just in case.

When someone touched his shoulder from behind, he shied like a nervous horse, then whirled around, the .38 steady in his hand, his trigger finger poised ready to waste the bastard.

"Mr. Yano?"

He relaxed as soon as he saw who it was. "Dammit, don't creep up on people like that, Ms. Roundtree. You could get yourself hurt." He tucked the pistol back in his waistband.

"You're already hurt." Frowning, she reached up to touch his wounded arm. "You should go to the emergency room."

"It's just a scratch, nothing to worry about." He grinned. "A Band-Aid or two and I'll be fine."

Her face remained grave. "That was a bullet, Mr. Yano. I was standing at the window and someone took a shot at me. Now do you believe I'm in danger?"

His grin faded. "Yeah, I do, only you don't need a private investigator. The police will handle the investigation. I'd only get in their way, and they tend to get a little jacked out of shape when that happens."

"Please, Mr. Yano." Her beautiful mix-and-match eyes were full of entreaty.

"I can't help you. The minute that bullet was fired, this became an active police case."

She took a step closer and placed one hand on his arm. "The police can't protect me twenty-four hours a day, but you could."

And what would her fiancé think of that? he wondered.

"Be my bodyguard, Mr. Yano. I don't want to die. I'll pay whatever you ask. Please."

Forget it, warned his common sense. *This lady's nothing but trouble. She's a flake. A beautiful flake, but a flake any way you slice it. And what's worse, she's engaged. Tell her to buzz off, Dix, old buddy. This case stinks to high heaven.*

"All right," Dixon agreed.

"Who knew the obituary was a fake?" After a tedious trek through the red-tape jungle at police headquarters followed by an equally irksome delay at the emergency room, Dixon had brought Alexandra back to his office, where cardboard and duct tape now blocked the view across the street. He handed her a mug of cocoa.

She took a sip, barely tasting it. Not even chocolate helped when depression was this profound. *Who knew the obituary was a fake?* What he really wanted was a list of suspects, a list of friends and family. "My mother. And my uncle, of course. My sister." She paused to take a calming breath. "And Mark."

"No one else?" The expression in Dixon Yano's soft brown eyes was even more comforting, more warming than the cup of hot chocolate she gripped between her hands.

She frowned. "Mandy probably told her husband, and Uncle Rex might have mentioned it to Aunt Virginia or my cousin Shelby."

"Mother, sister, brother-in-law, uncle, aunt, cousin, fiancé." Dixon counted them on his fingers. "A short list."

"It could have been an outsider, a stalker who followed me to your office." But she didn't really believe it.

"Maybe," he said. "How about motive? Who has a reason to want you dead?"

"Nobody!" Her protest was vehement.

Dixon raised an eyebrow. "Okay, then. Who benefits if you die? Who inherits?"

"I don't want to talk about this." Alex jumped to her

feet, sloshing cocoa down the front of her blouse. "Dammit!"

Dixon rescued the half-empty mug from her uncertain grasp and handed her a wad of tissues from the box on his desk.

Blinking back tears, she daubed at the stains. "Dammit," she said again, her voice shaking. "This blouse is silk." But Alex knew the cause of her upset wasn't a blouse.

Evidently Dixon did too. He folded her gently into his arms and held her until she calmed down.

Warm and comforting eyes. Warm and comforting arms. Alex relaxed. She felt safer in Dixon Yano's embrace than she'd felt in weeks. Why couldn't Mark hold her like this?

Mark. Mesmerized by the steady, reassuring beat of Dixon's heart, she'd forgotten about her fiancé. Reluctantly, Alex pulled herself free. "Sorry."

A rueful half smile tilted one corner of his mouth. "No problem."

Her heart skipped a beat at the expression on his face. Behind the kindness, the sympathy, she saw a hint of something else. Approval? Attraction?

She blinked, then deliberately shifted her gaze to the ring on her left hand, a nice, safe inanimate object.

If she were honest, she'd admit she was aware of him too. Dixon Yano's rugged good looks were very appealing.

Stay focused on the real problem, Alex. Somebody's trying to kill you. Irritated with herself, she paced the narrow office, pausing next to the makeshift cardboard windowpane. Now that the sun had gone down, the air penetrating the flimsy barrier was cold. She rocked back and forth, hugging herself against the chill while her thoughts ran in pointless circles. "What now?"

"First dinner, I think, and then bed."

She shot him a wary look, but he wasn't smirking at her. He wasn't even looking in her direction. He scowled instead at the scarred surface of his desk.

Another nice, safe inanimate object? she wondered, feeling obscurely cheered.

Alex jumped when he smacked one fist in the palm of the other hand like a baseball player testing his mitt. "Where will you be safest, though? You can't stay with any of the prime suspects, and you can't stay alone."

"My place," she surprised herself by saying. "I have an apartment over Gemini Gifts. No way in except through the shop."

"You can't stay alone," he repeated.

"I won't be alone because you'll be camping out down in the break room ready to protect me from the bad guys." Alex smiled. "I have a folding cot."

Dixon was scrunched up on the narrow cot, doing his best to get comfortable on a bed designed to accommodate a child. One support bar burrowed into his back just below the shoulder blades. A second elevated his knees. In between the two, the thin foam mattress dipped like a swaybacked nag.

He shifted, trying to relieve the pins and needles in his shoulders. He'd long since lost any feeling in his feet. They hung off the end of the mattress in the chilly limbo between the cot and the door.

Despite the discomfort, he must have dozed off, though, because it was after two when he shot upright, wide-awake, his heart slamming double time. He recognized the condition as fight-or-flight syndrome. But what had triggered it?

Stifling an idiotic urge to shout Who's there? Dixon slid quietly out of bed, his right hand reaching automatically for his gun. Barefoot, dressed only in a pair of black sweats, he slipped through the door of the break room. At first glance the shadowy shop, illuminated by a single overhead fixture in the office alcove, appeared empty. Then he saw her, a pale slim figure hovering near the back door. The hairs on his arms stood up. In a long flowing robe, she looked like the Ghost of Christmas Past. "Alexandra?"

"Shh." She held a finger to her lips. "I heard a noise out back. I think someone may be trying to break in."

Dixon moved noiselessly to her side. He could see her hands trembling, hear the catch in her voice.

A loud clang shattered the stillness, sending a fresh shot of adrenaline pumping through his bloodstream.

Alexandra jerked violently. "There it is again!"

Dixon motioned for her to move back, then eased the door open a crack, just far enough to accommodate the barrel of his gun and give him a narrow line of vision.

The harsh glare of the security light lit the paved area near the door. The night was cold and empty, the only sound the eerie whistle of the wind as it lashed the naked limbs of the poplars that formed a loose barrier between the parking lot and the railroad tracks.

Gooseflesh puckered the skin of his bare chest and arms, three parts attributable to the cold, one part a purely atavistic response to the unknown. What the hell had made that noise?

As Dixon edged through the door he caught a movement in his peripheral vision and whipped around just in time to see a raggedy, misshapen figure disappearing down the alley.

A bum. Just a bum.

And the sound? He scanned the area thoughtfully, his attention drawn to the Dumpster. He lifted the lid an experimental six inches or so and let it drop. The resulting sound was loud enough to wake the dead from their coffins.

Shouting threats and waving a mop, Alexandra rushed out the back door of the shop. She stopped abruptly, her fierce expression melting into confusion as she realized no enemy lurked within striking distance. Slowly she lowered her weapon. "What made that horrible racket?"

"Dumpster cover." Dixon demonstrated. "A bum was going through your trash."

"Myron?"

Dixon shrugged. "We didn't introduce ourselves."

"Myron's homeless. He's been hanging around for the past few months. I slip him food sometimes." She looked puzzled. "But I've never known him to prowl this late."

"Maybe he couldn't sleep." An affliction to which Dixon could relate.

TWO

"A wake would have been more appropriate," Alex complained, viewing her fellow party goers with a jaundiced eye. Not one of her mother's guests had mentioned either her obituary or its subsequent retraction in today's paper. She felt like the invisible woman.

"But you're not really dead," Regina pointed out with irrefutable logic. "And that's just as well; black is a wretched color on me." Her mother pressed a glass of punch into her hands. "Lighten up, sweetie. It's Christmas."

Alex started to take a sip, remembering in time Dixon's admonition that she avoid eating or drinking anything at the party. She frowned across the room. "Mother, that isn't Congressman Flanagan, is it?"

When Regina whipped around to look, Alex tipped the contents of her glass into a potted poinsettia.

"No, it's not. I was mistaken."

Spots of color highlighted her mother's cheekbones. "You must have been. I'd sooner invite the devil himself than that . . . that . . . Democrat!" She scanned the room, her fingers worrying at the fringe on her vest. "Who's the thug near the buffet table? I don't remember inviting him. Could he be one of Flanagan's flunkies?"

Alex waved a hand in a dismissive gesture. "No, that's Rocky, my bodyguard."

Regina frowned. "I thought you hired Dixon Yano."

"I did. But he had a court appearance this afternoon. Another case." She shrugged. "He knew he'd be late, so he enlisted Rocky to run interference until he gets here."

Her mother eyed Alex's alleged bodyguard dubiously. "Are you sure he's trustworthy? The man looks like a gangster."

"And drives like a maniac. We slewed sideways three times coming up your hill."

"You need studs," Regina said.

"Talking about me behind my back, Reggie?" Mark pulled Alex into a casual embrace and flashed her mother his hundred-megawatt grin.

Regina spared him a thin smile.

Alex prudently hid her own amusement. Her mother hated being called Reggie. Actually, she wasn't all that fond of Mark, no matter what he called her.

"We were talking about snow tires," Regina explained. "Alex's driver had trouble getting up the hill this evening."

Her mother's new log home sat on a hill overlooking Brunswick. The steep, winding drive was the price she paid for a spectacular view.

Regina turned to Alex. "Speaking of studs, shouldn't Dixon be here soon? You've met Dixon, haven't you, Mark?"

"Dixon who?"

Alex started to explain, but her mother cut her off. "You know, Dixon Yano."

"No, I don't know. Who's Dixon Yano?" Mark glanced from mother to daughter. "Any relation to old Hiroshi Yano, who owns most of Arrowhead Heights?"

Alex shook her head. "I have no idea who his relatives are. He's dark-complected, but he doesn't look Japanese."

"Dixon Yano is a private detective," Regina told Mark.

"Private investigator," Alex corrected.

Mark frowned. "What do you need with a PI, honey?"

Alex pulled her hair behind her ear. "Look at the side of my face, Mark. Someone took a shot at me yesterday."

Mark brushed her right cheek. "These look like cuts, not bullet wounds."

Did he sound disappointed? Alex studied his face for a moment, then gave herself an angry little mental shake. She didn't seriously suspect Mark, did she?

"Bullet wounds? What's this? I thought you said you weren't hurt!" Regina's voice rose shrilly. Several of her guests turned to stare.

Alex shook her head. "I wasn't. A few scratches. With my hair down, they don't even show. I caught a little flying glass. Dixon's the one who was shot."

"How is he?" Regina still sounded upset.

"Sore, but not incapacitated. The bullet just grazed his arm."

"There you go." Mark snapped his fingers. "He was probably the target all along. PIs are always ruffling people's feathers. You're getting paranoid, honey." He gave Alex's shoulders a squeeze.

"Paranoid?" Regina's lip curled. "What about the threatening letter? The mugging in the mall? The exploding reindeer?"

Mark's smile held a hint of condescension. "A series of coincidences, Reggie."

"If I stuck a 'series of coincidences' like that in a mystery novel, my editor would throw a tantrum." Regina's eyes snapped with annoyance.

Alex racked her brain for a way to defuse the situation. Much more of Mark's interpretation and her mother was the one who'd throw a tantrum. She scanned the big, two-story living room, looking for a diversion.

Like a couple of impatient vultures, her brother-in-law, Tom, and her sister, Mandy, were circling Sadie Silverberg, Regina's agent.

Tom Sutton was an excellent proctologist and a wretched wannabe writer. He'd recently finished a manuscript he called *Complications*, a combination medical thriller/horror novel in which his hero accidentally received a transfusion of vampire blood during a routine hemorrhoid operation. He'd already been turned down by eleven agents. Apparently he was going for an even dozen.

"Emergency at two o'clock." Alex indicated the impending calamity with a jerk of her head.

"Oh, Lordy." Regina set off on an interception course.

"What's the deal?" Mark asked.

Alex sighed. Tom was a nice guy . . . if only he would limit his writing to prescriptions. "Tom wrote a . . ." She let her explanation trail off when she realized Mark wasn't listening. His attention was riveted on something across the room. She followed his gaze to the group near the fireplace. Nothing exciting there. "Mark?" She tapped his arm. "Do you want to try the buffet?" As soon as she said it, she remembered Dixon's warning. Okay, fine. She wouldn't eat anything. She'd just shove the food back and forth across her plate.

"I'm not hungry."

"Did you eat before you came? Is that why you were late?"

"No, something came up. Business. At the office." He sounded distracted.

Admit it, Alex. He sounds like he's lying.

"There's Eileen." He gave Alex's shoulders another squeeze before releasing her. "I'd better go make nice."

Eileen Loomis, part of the group near the fireplace, was the wife of the senior partner of Mark's law firm.

"Want some company?" Alexandra's offer was half-hearted. She'd never cared for either Loomis or his wife.

"No thanks, honey." Mark grinned. "You might cramp my style. I plan to lay it on thick. There's a part-nership coming up, you know."

Alex watched in irritation as he sauntered over to greet Eileen, the expression on his handsome face so charming, it ought to come with a warning label. He whispered something in the older woman's ear and she slapped playfully at his arm.

Alex clenched her hands into fists. Why did Mark think he had to play office politics? He was a good law-yer. Wasn't ability alone enough to secure a partnership?

Turning away in disgust, Alex surveyed the enormous living area. Regina Roundtree's tree-trimming party was an annual event, a clever way to get her tree decorated and pay off her social obligations all in one fell swoop. One group of guests was putting the finishing touches on the tree while another had gathered around the piano, where Sadie Silverberg was pounding out "God Rest Ye, Merry Gentlemen" with all the verve of a born-again Christian. Alex opted to join the singers.

Dixon leaned against the doorbell. Even through the door he heard the chimes ring out, sandwiched in between one "comfort and joy" and another. But as the seconds passed and no one let him in, he began to suspect he was the only one who *had* heard the chimes. He pressed the doorbell a second time, propping himself wearily against the door frame as he waited. His injured arm throbbed in time with the piano.

"Hey, there! Do I know you?"

Dixon twisted his head around to see a perky little redhead wearing a faux-fur coat and industrial-strength makeup.

She drew back crimson lips in a smile as predatory as any crocodile's. "We haven't met, have we? I'd have remembered." As she stepped forward to extend her hand her earrings, garish baubles shaped like miniature Christmas ornaments, caught the light. "I'm Shelby Winters, Regina's niece." She squeezed his hand.

"Dixon Yano."

"Friend of Regina's?" The look she gave him held a speculative edge.

"Acquaintance."

"You know my cousins, then? Alex and Mandy?"

"I know Alexandra."

She laughed. "Of course you do. The good-looking guys always know Alex."

Inside, the carolers launched into "The Twelve Days of Christmas."

Dixon leaned on the doorbell for a third time.

The redhead moved a step closer, idly stroking the soft leather of his jacket sleeve with one narrow, beringed hand. "I work with Alex and Mandy at Gemini Gifts. What's your line?"

"Private investigations."

Shelby batted her lashes. "Ooh! Like on TV. How exciting! Tell me more."

The sudden rush of warmth and noise behind him told Dixon someone had finally opened the door.

"Dixon Yano?"

Turning, he saw Regina Roundtree. Alexandra stood next to her mother, a smile on her lovely face, an engaging sparkle in her eyes.

"Mrs. Roundtree."

"Regina, please." Regina Roundtree clasped his hand warmly. "It's good to see you again. The interview you gave me last summer helped enormously with my last book."

Shelby inserted herself in the gap between Dixon and the door, placing a proprietary hand on his forearm. "Dixon was just telling me he's a PI. Isn't that fascinating? I don't think I ever met a detective before." She slanted a soulful look at him.

Alexandra raised an eyebrow, her voice carefully polite. "You two are together?"

Dixon felt guilty despite having done nothing to feel guilty about. "No, I . . . we just met. Right here on the porch. I rang the bell, but . . ." No matter what he said, it sounded like an excuse.

"Dixon and I had a nice little chat, didn't we?"

Shelby patted his arm. "The life of a private detective must be so exciting. I bet you have dozens of thrilling stories, and I'm dying to hear them all."

"Well, Shelby dear, we're all going to be dying soon . . . of pneumonia. Come in, you two. It's freezing." Regina drew them inside and shut the door.

Shelby clung to Dixon's arm, her slender fingers clutching him like talons.

"Excuse me." He freed himself, shrugged out of his jacket, and slung it over his shoulder.

Fanning her lashes, Shelby promptly reattached herself to his sweatered arm. "So, tell me, Dixon, do you carry a gun?"

"Now and then." Ginger from *Gilligan's Island*. That's who she reminded him of. Unfortunately, he'd always preferred Mary Ann. Dixon shot the Roundtree women an imploring look. He didn't want to be rude, but . . .

Regina moved swiftly to the rescue. "Shelby, would you do me a favor? Run Dixon's coat upstairs and add it to the pile in the master bedroom? Thank you, dear."

Shelby opened her mouth, then shut it again as her aunt took the coat from Dixon and shoved it into her arms. Casting one final smoldering glance in Dixon's direction, she retreated.

"Such a friendly little thing," Regina commented once Shelby was safely out of earshot.

"Friendly." A faint sneer crossed Alexandra's face.

"I owe you one, Regina. Thanks." He shook his hostess's hand again, then turned to Alexandra. "How's it going? Anyone ask you about the obituary or mention the excitement yesterday?"

"The obituary I know about. But excitement? This

sounds promising." Smiling broadly, she lifted an eyebrow. "I think you're mistaking me for my sister, though. I'm Amanda Sutton, Alex's twin."

Dixon studied her closely as they shook hands. "I should have noticed right away. Alexandra's left eye is hazel and her right eye is blue. You're reversed."

Amanda tapped his arm approvingly. "Very good. Most people don't pick up on that. Alex and I are mirror-image twins, not true identicals."

"So where *is* Alexandra?"

"Five golden rings," Alex sang, then fell silent. Someone was watching her. A quick glance toward the hearth told her Mark was still busy charming the pants off Eileen Loomis, so who . . .

Just inside the entryway, Dixon Yano stood next to Amanda and her mother, but he wasn't looking at them. He was looking at her. She met his gaze. Time slowed, then stopped for the space of three endless heartbeats.

One . . .

She liked his looks. He'd shaved since she'd last seen him and exchanged the T-shirt he'd worn all day for a sweater. By some miracle of mousse and sheer determination, he'd even managed to smooth his unruly brown hair back into a semblance of order. He looked gorgeous. Yet even in his previously rumpled state, Dixon Yano had been extraordinarily attractive. Maybe not *GQ* handsome like Mark with his Armani suits and blow-dried hair, but good-looking in a more rugged, more primal, more swashbuckling way, like Mel Gibson in *Braveheart* or Adrian Paul in *Highlander*.

Two . . .

She liked his style. Yes, he was sexy as all get-out, but he'd also proved he was a man she could depend on. After the police had come up empty in their search for her would-be assailant yesterday, Dixon had answered all their questions, then driven her to the emergency room, where he'd made sure she was taken care of before he would consent to be treated himself. He'd been calm, cool, and decisive—even in a crisis.

Three . . .

She liked his determination, a determination apparent now in the stubborn set of his jaw. She felt confident that her bodyguard would keep her safe or die trying.

Across a sea of milling guests, his dark eyes burned into hers, compelling, mesmerizing. A strange emotion twisted in Alex's chest. She felt breathless with anticipation, as if something truly momentous were about to happen.

Slowly, a smile tugged at the corners of Dixon Yano's mouth, softening his rugged features and melting her heart. Time resumed.

THREE

Alex trembled violently. Her cheeks burned. Was he still staring at her? She couldn't look.

". . . and a partridge in a pear tree!" finished the group around the piano.

"Why aren't you singing?" Sadie asked. "You're the only one of this bunch who can carry a tune."

Alex blinked several times in rapid succession. Why wasn't she singing? She opened her mouth, but couldn't seem to find the words to answer the question.

Sadie looked at her oddly.

Alex shrugged and shook her head, feeling disoriented and slightly panicky, like an actress who'd suddenly forgotten all her lines.

His face kept getting in the way. His eyes. The saddest eyes she'd ever seen. Even when he smiled. Especially when he smiled.

Dixon Yano's face. Dixon Yano's eyes. How strange. For a moment there she hadn't been able to tear her gaze from his. Now she was afraid to look at him at all, afraid of what she might see in his face, afraid of what he might see in hers.

She caught a flash of movement from the corner of her eye. Glancing across the room, she saw her mother waving, trying to catch her attention. The light of the big chandelier danced off the half-dozen gold bracelets that jangled on Regina's arm.

Alex blinked again. Dixon was still there, but he wasn't staring at her anymore. His dark head was bent toward Mandy. She said something and he threw his head back, his laugh ringing out over the buzz of the crowd. What was so funny? Alex wondered, conscious suddenly of a dull throb at her temples.

"Alex?"

She jumped. Mark had slipped up on her unawares. "What?"

Sadie banged out the opening chords of "We Three Kings."

Frowning, Mark shook his head. "Not here. Too noisy." He pulled her away from the carolers.

"What is it?"

He nodded toward the corner. "See Ed Loomis sitting over there? He looks bored, and that's not good. Go spread a little Christmas cheer. He likes you."

"But I don't like him. The man is second cousin to an octopus." Alex shuddered as she remembered the feel of Ed Loomis's doughy white fingers. He'd groped her once in the hot tub at the fitness center, then pretended it was an accident.

Mark squeezed her hands. "He's my boss, Alex, and there's a partnership coming up soon. Do it for me, honey."

Do *what* for him? She shot him a wary look.

Mark laughed at her dubious expression and gave her a quick, reassuring hug. "Just be nice to Loomis, okay? The least you can do is save him from that brother-in-law of yours. Old Tom's probably giving Ed a blow-by-blow of his last colostomy."

Tom did seem to be involved in an animated monologue, and since the only two topics in his conversational repertoire were bowels and vampires . . .

Alex sighed in resignation. "Okay, I'll rescue your boss if you'll see what my mother wants. She was trying to flag me down a minute ago."

"Sure. Whatever."

"Polyps can lead to bowel cancer," Tom said, staring hard at his captive audience. "When was your last rectal exam, Ed?"

Alex tapped her sister's husband on the shoulder. "Mandy's looking for you."

Tom swiveled his head, scanning the room. "She is? I haven't moved for the last ten minutes. Ed and I have been sitting here discussing the importance of preventative medicine, haven't we, Ed?"

The lawyer grunted noncommittally and took another gulp of his whiskey. From the looks of him, it wasn't his first drink of the evening. Or his second.

Tom shoved his glasses back up the bridge of his nose. "Where'd you see Mandy? Did she say what she wanted?"

"Near the door, and no, she didn't, but I think it might have something to do with your book."

"Oh!" He jumped to his feet. "I bet she talked to that Silverman woman."

"Silverberg," Alex called after his retreating back.

"Thanks," Loomis muttered, slurring the word.

She turned to him reluctantly.

"Have a seat," he said, leering up at her and patting the cushion next to him. His fingers looked like fat white sausages against the red velvet upholstery.

Alex's smile felt stiff and false. "Maybe later. I promised Mother I'd check something in the kitchen first."

She beat a hasty retreat before he could cross-examine her about her supposed errand. She was a lousy liar, no match for a lawyer, not even a lawyer who was three sheets to the wind.

The kitchen was an oasis of relative quiet once she closed the door. She peered out the window into the darkness. Snow was falling, but not heavily.

Her substitute bodyguard had left shortly after Dixon's arrival. She hoped he hadn't wrapped his old boat of a Ford around a power pole on the way down the hill. According to Rocky, snow tires were for sissies.

She sat down at the little drop-leaf table next to the bay window. If ever a woman needed time alone, time to think, time to order her priorities . . .

What happened back there? One minute she'd been counting down the twelve days of Christmas and the next she was caught up in this whole "Strangers in the Night" thing. She stared down in dismay at the diamond solitaire adorning her ring finger. She was engaged, dammit. She was engaged to a highly eligible man—handsome, charming, successful. So why was her heart racing out of control at a look from someone else?

Dixon Yano. That face. Those eyes.

With a groan, she buried her face in her hands. *I must be going crazy.*

The door banged open and she glanced up, startled, suddenly remembering Dixon's advice about staying in a crowd.

"Oh, there you are!" Ed Loomis stumbled over his own feet and nearly fell. He caught himself on the edge of the table, blowing whiskey fumes in her face and slopping the contents of his half-empty glass down the front of her sweater. "Sorry about that. Here, let me help."

"I can manage," she said curtly. Boss be damned. The man was a pig.

Brushing aside her protests, he grabbed a dish towel and mopped enthusiastically at her sweater, managing to fondle both her breasts in the process. His fingers weren't sausages, she decided. They were maggots, bloated white maggots.

"It's fine. I'll go change into something of my mother's." Shoving his hands away, she shrank back in disgust, but there was nowhere to go. He had her pinned in a corner.

"Need any help?" His leering red face repulsed her.

"No!" He backed off a pace at the sharpness of her tone. Hoping to take advantage of his momentary retreat, she tried to slide around him, but he lurched back into her path, cutting off her only escape route.

"That doesn't sound very frien'ly," Loomis commented, and grabbed her. The naked lust on his face sent a shiver down Alex's spine and the alcohol on his breath made her stomach roll, but even more disgusting were his fat white fingers. They seemed to be everywhere, crawling over her arms, wriggling under her sweater, sliding up her neck and along her cheeks.

"Stop it!" She struggled frantically, trying to maneuver herself out of the corner, trying to push him away, trying to get her knee up where it would do some good.

Ed Loomis was drunk and twenty pounds overweight, but he was also twice her size. Alex knew she couldn't overpower him, but she wasn't going down without a fight. Kicking out blindly, she nailed his shin.

He grunted in surprise, then retaliated with a slap that made her ears ring.

Tears sprang to her eyes. Lashing out reflexively, she dug her nails into the loose wattle of his second chin. She grinned fiercely at his yip of pain.

"I love a woman with spirit," he muttered as he twisted her arms up behind her back. "Relax and enjoy it, baby. The missus was enjoying herself with Mark a while ago. What's sauce for the goose is sauce for the gander. And vice versa." His chuckle sounded like sludge gurgling through sewer pipes.

What did he mean about Mark "enjoying" himself? Was he referring to the cozy tête-à-tête near the fireplace? Or something else?

"I'll scream," she threatened, her voice vibrating with loathing.

"I don't think so." His arms were a vise that held her imprisoned against him so tightly she could scarcely move, barely breathe. "You don't want to spoil your mama's nice party." He tightened his grip as if to emphasize his point.

The pain was incredible, but it was the smile on his face that curdled her blood.

Alex drew a painful breath, fighting for enough air to make good on her threat, but before she could utter a sound, his mouth engulfed hers in a sloppy kiss.

She writhed like a madwoman, but with his mouth

devouring hers, the only sound she could make was a mewling whine, not loud enough to be audible over the noise of the party.

Suddenly she was free and Ed Loomis was sitting on the tiled floor six feet away, nursing his jaw.

"I think you owe the lady an apology." Dixon Yano reached down with one hand to drag the lawyer to his feet.

"Who the hell are you?"

"A man doing his job." Dixon's voice was colder than the wind that shivered along the eaves outside.

"It's your job to assault people?" Loomis ran his tongue along the inside of his cheek, checking for damage.

"Not people, just drunken rapists."

Loomis's face turned purple. "That's slander!" he blustered, though it came out sounding more like "schlander." "Def'mation of character! I'm going to sue your shorts off."

"Be my guest." Dixon's expression was even colder than his voice. "But if this goes to court, I'll testify to the fact I caught you molesting the woman I'm being paid to protect."

"M'lesting her?" Loomis spluttered.

"Sure looked that way to me."

"I swear to God, all I did was kiss her. Just a frien'ly Christmas kiss."

Dixon glanced pointedly around the room. "I don't see any mistletoe. You see any mistletoe, Alexandra?"

Alex shook her head.

Dixon bent nearer, his voice gentle. "Are you all right?"

She nodded, but she couldn't stop the tear that slid down her cheek.

He wiped the moisture from her face with his fingertips, then balled his hand into a fist. Slowly, he turned to Loomis. "Men who manhandle women really pull my chain. If you want to leave with all your teeth, I suggest you get the hell out of here before I count to three. One . . ."

"I—I—" Warily, never taking his eyes from the younger man, Loomis backed away.

"Two . . ."

Turning, Loomis fumbled frantically with the door-knob. He shot a nervous glance back over his shoulder.

"Three." Dixon's smile was grim.

With a whimper of fear, Loomis whipped out of sight, slamming the door behind him.

Alex slumped into a chair, all the strength draining from her body. "Thank you," she whispered.

"Who the hell was that?"

"Edward Loomis. The senior partner in my fiancé's law firm." She closed her eyes. "He got carried away. He's drunk."

"He's slime."

"That too." She stared at her own white-knuckled fists.

"Are you sure you're all right?" he persisted, touching her shoulder tentatively.

Alex nodded. "Other than a little residual shakiness and the fact I smell like a distillery. He slopped whiskey on my sweater," she explained. "The dry cleaner's going to get rich off me this week."

He lifted her chin so she was forced to look him in the eye. "Do you want to go home?"

She was still shaky. A deep breath helped. So did the tender expression in his eyes. "Yes, I think so. Would you collect my coat while I explain to my mother?"

"Sure." Dixon didn't like the haunted expression in her eyes. She looked as fragile as a glass ornament. If he had been doing his job, that Loomis jerk wouldn't have dared to lay a finger on her. Attempted molestation and attempted murder all in the same week. No wonder Alexandra Roundtree looked as if she would shatter under the slightest pressure.

He wove his way through the party goers and up the stairs. The festivities were still going strong, though the party seemed to have shifted into low gear. Several couples were dancing to "White Christmas."

Upstairs, a ruby-red Turkish carpet swallowed the sound of his footsteps. The interior walls were hung with a collection of colorful antique quilts that was probably worth more than he earned in a good year. Evidently mystery writers were well compensated for their work.

To his surprise, the heavy wooden door to the master bedroom was locked. He rattled the knob a second time just to be sure.

"Just a minute," came the muffled response from inside. A man's voice.

Dixon froze with his hand on the doorknob. What the hell was going on?

A few seconds later the door swung open. Mark Jordan stood there, tucking his shirt back into the waistband of his trousers. He backed away from the door, allowing Dixon to enter. "Sorry. I was using the john in here. There's no lock on the bathroom door, and I didn't want to get caught with my pants down." His smile was designed to charm, but it failed to impress Dixon.

"I came for Alexandra's coat."

"*Alexandra's* coat? Who are you?" Jordan eyed him suspiciously.

"Dixon Yano. I work for Ms. Roundtree."

A supercilious smile played at the corners of Jordan's mouth. "Oh, right. The private dick."

Dixon met Jordan's smirk with a stony stare.

Jordan was the first to look away.

Score one for the hired gun.

Jordan cleared his throat. "Don't tell me Alex is leaving already." He frowned. "I wanted to introduce her to Bill and Maureen Dennison, influential new clients of the firm."

"I think she's had about all of the firm she can stand for one night. Your boss just made a very clumsy pass at her."

A petulant frown still creasing his forehead, Mark Jordan studied himself in the mirror above the dresser, then ran a hand over his already sleek head. "You'd think a grown woman could handle one amorous drunk," he muttered.

Dixon had a sudden murderous impulse to sink his fingers in that shiny hair and slam Mark Jordan's classic chiseled features into the wall. "Does Alexandra normally carry a purse?" he asked instead. He'd located his leather jacket and her coat, the same one she'd worn to his office earlier, but the big black leather purse wasn't among those stacked on the bed.

"Sometimes. Other times she shoves her wallet in her pocket." Jordan seemed fascinated by his own reflection. He rubbed at a smudge just below his lower lip.

The wallet was right where Jordan had predicted it would be. Smug bastard. Staring with loathing at the back of Jordan's perfectly styled blond head, Dixon wondered how many times the lawyer had driven Alexandra home, how many times he'd stayed the night in the apartment over Gemini Gifts.

Clenching his teeth as he tried to suppress the image of Alexandra in Jordan's arms, Dixon glanced down, noticing something that had slipped between two of the lacy pillows piled at the head of the bed. He bent to retrieve the shiny bauble, an earring shaped like a miniature Christmas ornament.

Jordan went very still. He wasn't primping any longer. He wasn't even looking at himself. All his attention was trained on the reflection of the gaudy earring in Dixon's hand.

What excuse would Jordan make, Dixon wondered, if he said he had to use the john? The redhead was hiding in the bathroom. He was sure of it.

Damn it all to hell and back, this Jordan character was one pitiful excuse for a man. Cheating on his fiancée. Cheating on his fiancée with her own cousin. Cheating on his fiancée with her own cousin in said fiancée's mother's bedroom. The whole messy scenario played like something off a damn soap opera.

He dropped the earring in the center of the bedspread. "Looks like somebody lost something."

"What?" Jordan pretended to notice it for the first time.

"An earring, I think."

"Probably Reggie's." Mark Jordan's laugh was forced. "Her collection of costume jewelry rivals her collection of hats."

"She must have dropped it when she was getting dressed."

"Probably." A self-satisfied smirk twisted Jordan's mouth.

Once again Dixon felt an almost uncontrollable urge to slap the jerk around. He was no bully, never had been, but every damn thing about Jordan rubbed him the wrong way. Everything up to and including the fact that he was engaged to Alexandra Roundtree.

"It's snowing harder." Alex eyed the flurries in dismay.

"Just in time for Christmas." Dixon helped her down the steps of the deck.

"I hate snow. At least I hate driving in it."

"Don't worry. My Jeep has studded snow tires. I'll get you home safely."

Safe. That word again. She placed her gloved hand on his sleeve. "Thanks."

He stopped, staring down at her for a moment in silence. Then he covered her hand with his own. "Don't mention it. You're going to be fine. I promise."

She smiled faintly. "I hope you're right, Mr. Yano."

"Not Mr. Yano."

"What?"

"The name's Dixon."

Her smile grew a little wider. "And I'm Alexandra, Alex if you prefer."

"Alexandra," he repeated, then again, softly, "Alexandra."

Her name sounded almost exotic the way he said it.

Dixon negotiated the hill without incident in his four-wheel-drive vehicle. Alexandra must have felt secure with him behind the wheel. Either that or she was so terrified she couldn't bear to watch the road. At any rate, she leaned against the headrest and shut her eyes.

He tuned the radio to a local soft-rock station and she began humming along to a song. They were at the city limits before either of them said a word.

"You—" started Alex.

"How—" Dixon began at the same time. "Sorry. You first."

"It wasn't anything important. I was just wondering how you ended up with a Japanese name. As I mentioned when we first met, you don't look Japanese."

He smiled. "My mom's Swedish. Dad's half–Heinz fifty-seven, half-Japanese."

"Are you related to Hiroshi Yano?"

"He's my grandfather. You know him?"

"No, Mark just asked me if there was a connection."

Dixon's tone was dry. "Grandfather has Tollman, Loomis, and Taylor on retainer, though after tonight I may suggest he take his business elsewhere."

"Ed Loomis is a pig." She drew a long, unsteady breath. "What were you going to say?"

Dammit, the quaver was back in her voice again. He hadn't meant to remind her of Loomis. "Just wondered if you wanted to stop off at the grocery store for anything before we head home." He wished the words back as soon as they were spoken. He'd made it sound as if they were living together. Which they were, of course, though not in the way he'd accidentally implied.

But if Alexandra thought he was presuming, she

didn't mention it. She simply shook her head no and subsided into silence.

Was she brooding over the ugly episode with Loomis? Or worrying about what conclusions people might leap to when they learned she'd hired a live-in bodyguard? "What did your fiancé say when you told him I'd be protecting you around the clock?" He pulled into the center turn lane on Idaho Avenue and flicked on his right-turn signal. Enough snow had fallen to blur the lines marking the lanes. The windshield wipers clickclacked monotonously as he waited for her response.

"Nothing."

The red light changed to a green arrow and he turned onto Oregon. Downtown traffic was light this time of night. A couple bars were still open, one theater, the Basque restaurant across from the auto shop, not much else.

"Pretty open-minded guy, your fiancé." He passed his office. Gemini Gifts was four blocks south on the same side of the street.

"I didn't actually tell him you were staying at my place." She shrugged. "The subject never came up. Turn up here at the corner of Fourth Avenue. If you park in the lot behind the store, we can go in the back door."

The decorations at this end of the street put his block to shame. In addition to the cheesy lamppost angels put up by the city, all the store owners had hung their own decorations. The place was ablaze with tinsel and blinking lights. Predictably, Gemini Gifts sparkled even more intensely than its neighbors.

He turned left on Fourth and pulled into the public lot that filled the half block between the stores that lined

Oregon and the railroad tracks. A bum—Myron?—was digging through the Dumpster behind Marker's Fine Furniture. Otherwise, the place was deserted.

He parked close to the building. Alexandra got out on the passenger's side. Dixon locked the Jeep before following her to the door.

She looked up at his approach, her eyes huge.

"What is it?" Tension knotted his gut.

"The door's open, and I know I locked it when I left. I remember because I had trouble getting the key out. It sticks sometimes."

"Stay back. Someone may be inside."

"Maybe we should call the police," she whispered.

Dixon trained the pencil flashlight from his key chain on the lock. "No sign of forced entry. Whoever it was had a key. Are you positive you locked up? It's been a pretty traumatic day. It's easy to screw up when you're upset."

"I'm positive."

"Okay." He handed her his keys. "Call the cops. The cell phone's in the car."

"Don't go in by yourself. Promise me."

"I won't. The cops'd have my license if I tainted a crime scene. Did you touch the doorknob?"

She shook her head. "I was too scared to go inside once I realized that the door was already open a crack." She stared at the knob, shivering uncontrollably.

"The cops," he reminded her.

"Right." She seemed to pull herself together. "Right."

He watched her start toward the Jeep before he loped over to the Dumpster at the other end of the block.

The bum was still there prodding through the trash, apparently in search of cans.

"Hey, fella! How long you been out here?"

The man glanced up at Dixon's approach, his eyes rheumy and vague. "What year is it?"

It took a second or two for Dixon to realize the bum was laughing, not gasping his last breath. The closer he got, the worse the smell, a noxious blend of garbage, filth, and vomit. Dixon wasn't sure if it was emanating from the Dumpster or the bum. Maybe both.

"You see anybody hanging around the gift shop earlier tonight?"

"What's it worth to you?"

Dixon pulled a ten from his wallet. "This jog your memory?"

The old man scratched himself with the dowel he'd been using to poke through the trash. "I can't say for sure. It's still a little hazy."

Dixon shrugged. He didn't know whether the old man had seen anything or not, but he wasn't in the mood for playing games or shelling out any more cash. "The lady just called the cops. Talk to me or talk to them. Take your choice."

"Lord o' mercy, boy, not the cops. They'll drag me down to the shelter and I'll have all them damn do-gooders prayin' over me like I was Jack the Ripper." He snatched the ten bucks and stashed it in an inside pocket of his voluminous overcoat. "Whaddaya wanna know?"

"Just if you saw anybody suspicious hanging around the back of the gift store."

"I dunno as I'd call him suspicious."

"Who? Who did you see?"

"You're not gonna believe me." Using the end of the

grubby dowel, the bum scratched a question mark in the snow covering the pavement.

"Who?"

The old duffer's lips stretched in a toothless grin that was scary enough to give a grown man nightmares. He cackled like a Halloween witch. "Santy Claus," he said.

FOUR

"Santa Claus?" Officer Rios arched an eyebrow. "Gimme a break."

Dixon frowned. "I know it sounds crazy, but I'd swear the bum was telling the truth."

"Why? Because you paid him ten bucks? Old Myron'd tell you it was ninety degrees in the shade if that's what he thought you wanted to hear."

"That's the thing, Cesar. He didn't know what I wanted to hear."

Officer Rios leaned against the cash desk near the back of the main showroom at Gemini Gifts. He'd checked the place thoroughly, but found no evidence of an intruder, no sign of a break-in. "My guess is you left the door open yourself, Ms. Roundtree. It happens all the time. People get in a hurry."

"She remembers locking the door, Cesar. She remembers specifically because the lock gave her a hard time."

Alexandra chewed at her lip. "Maybe it was the same Santa."

"What same Santa?"

Dixon slapped his thigh. "That's it! I bet you're right." He turned to Cesar. "Alexandra mentioned the mugging in her statement yesterday. Remember? Last week in the mall someone dressed in a Santa suit snatched her purse."

Cesar nodded thoughtfully. "Yeah, a mugger in a Santa suit. Okay. Makes sense. Maybe old Myron wasn't spinning fairy tales or having drunken delusions either. You've got no sign of forced entry. But then, if Santa got her purse, he would have her address and her keys too. Still doesn't explain why nothing's missing, though. You're sure nothing's missing?"

Alexandra shrugged, looking around helplessly at the well-stocked store. Gemini Gifts was filled to the rafters with Christmas merchandise, everything from ornate music boxes from Switzerland to hand-stitched Christmas quilts from the Appalachians. "It's impossible to say for certain, but I know all of the more expensive items are still here. And upstairs, everything seems to be just the way I left it too. The antique silver's accounted for and my few pieces of good jewelry."

"So why did he break in?" Cesar Rios stared at a crystal angel that hung suspended above a Nativity scene. "And why did he leave the door hanging open when he left?"

"He had to leave in a hurry?" suggested Alexandra. "Maybe he heard Myron banging around in the Dumpster and panicked."

"Or maybe it's a subtle threat," Dixon said. "Maybe

he wants you to know he can get in whenever he feels
like it. He wants you to feel vulnerable."

Alexandra's laugh was shaky. "If so, he succeeded."

"Get the locks changed first thing tomorrow," Cesar
advised. "You should have done that already. I'm off
duty"—he checked his watch—"as of ten minutes ago.
But I'll have the officer on graveyard keep an eye on the
place for the rest of the night. I honestly don't expect
jolly old Saint Nick to do an encore performance, but
with the crazies you never know."

"I'll be here," Dixon told him. "Anybody wants to
get at her, they're going to have to go through me."

Cesar shot him a look.

Dixon knew what he was thinking. Since when did a
class act like Alexandra Roundtree hang with a gumshoe
like Dixon Yano? Since never, but he wasn't about to give
Cesar the satisfaction of hearing him admit it.

"Thanks for responding so quickly, man." Dixon
didn't actually shove Cesar toward the door, but his intent was clear.

"Glad to be of service." Ignoring Dixon's unsubtle
hint, Cesar turned his attention to Alexandra. "Ms.
Roundtree?" He took her right hand between his two big
paws and gave her one of the most blatantly sensual
smiles Dixon had ever seen. Cesar fancied himself Brunswick's answer to Antonio Banderas.

Gritting his teeth, Dixon remembered all the times in
the past he'd watched in grudging admiration as Cesar
had used similar moves to charm a susceptible female.

"Yes?" Alexandra's lips curved in a smile.

Was it just Dixon's imagination or did she sound
breathless? If so, he could hardly blame her. She

wouldn't be the first woman—or the hundredth—to fall victim to Cesar's Latin charm.

"If there's anything I can do to help, let me know." Cesar's voice was a throaty purr that put Dixon's hackles up. "You can reach me through the department or call me at home. My number's in the book." He released her hand slowly, as if he were memorizing the texture of her skin. As he turned to go he flicked a gloating sideways glance at Dixon.

Grimly, Dixon wondered how much jail time old Judge Brenner'd give him for assaulting a cop. Anything short of a week would be worth it.

Alexandra's soft voice intruded on his speculations. "Thanks again, Officer Rios. It's good to know there are men like you protecting the city."

Oh, puh-leeze!

Alexandra escorted Dixon's former friend to the back door.

Dixon stayed behind, only half listening to their conversation. Cesar didn't miss a trick; the man was a shameless flirt. Not that it mattered this time. Alexandra Roundtree wasn't interested in either Cesar Rios or Dixon Yano. She already had a fiancé, scuzzball that he was.

Dixon stared glumly at the crystal angel, thinking his mother might like something like that for Christmas until he noticed the discreet price sticker on the sole of the angel's bare foot. Hot damn! Not for fifty bucks, she wouldn't. He stepped back a pace to put a careful distance between himself and the fragile gewgaw. Like the sign above the door said: You break it, you buy it.

"Watch out!" Alexandra warned.

He spun around on his heel.

"You nearly backed right over me." Her eyes were dancing as if she found his clumsiness amusing, even endearing.

Endearing was good. "Sorry," he mumbled, shoving his hands in his pockets. "All this stuff"—he eyed the merchandise warily—"makes me nervous. I'm scared to death I'll accidentally break something." Something expensive.

She nodded, smiling. "Most men react that way. Mandy and I call it the bull-in-the-china-shop syndrome. You seem to have a worse case than most, perhaps because you're bigger than most." She broke off, her cheeks flushing a delicate pink. "Larger, I mean. That is, taller." She stopped, breathing hard, as if she'd just run a sprint.

Suddenly Dixon felt a whole lot more at ease. "My mom says Swensons come in only two sizes, extra large and the giant, economy size."

Alexandra didn't ask which he was. She caught her lower lip between her teeth. "I'm having second thoughts about your sleeping on the cot. I know you didn't get much rest last night."

Was this her way of kicking him out? He cleared his throat. "Not a problem. Really. I don't require a lot of sleep." And wouldn't get much, either. Not knowing she was right upstairs.

She glanced sideways at him. "I was thinking you could sleep upstairs with me." The pink in her cheeks deepened to rose. "I mean, upstairs in the apartment." He could see the pulse fluttering in her throat.

He made her nervous. So either she was scared spitless of him or she found him threatening for some other reason. Like maybe she was attracted to him despite the fact she was engaged to Jordan. Dixon felt the tiniest flicker of hope.

"That would work, I guess." He sounded pretty darn cheerful for a man whose odds of getting any sleep were narrowing by the second.

"This way." She preceded him up the enclosed staircase at the back of the shop.

Dixon found his thoughts wandering as he watched her mount the stairs. Not many women could wear those baggy menswear trousers without looking frumpy, but Ms. Roundtree was an exception. Good glutes, he decided. That was her secret.

"I hope Officer Rios was right about that creep not coming back again tonight," she said, refocusing his thoughts on the case.

"I'm sure he is, but I wouldn't feel right leaving you here on your own."

The door at the top of the staircase led directly into the living room, where they'd been cooped up for most of the day. Dixon eyed the sofa dubiously. It was fairly comfortable and, thankfully, longer than the cot, but it was also narrow. Too narrow. He'd have to sleep on his side all night. Probably wake up with a crick in his neck.

Alexandra tugged at his sleeve. "Come see your room."

"My room?"

"The spare room. Mandy's before she married Tom."

Though decidedly feminine, with its chintz and ruffles, the room was big, the bed king size. "This is great. Thanks."

She smiled. "Better than your feet hanging over the end of that cot anyway. The bathroom's through here." She opened a door. "It connects the two bedrooms so you'll have to make sure both doors are locked if you need privacy. You can use the shower first, if you'd like."

Dixon shook his head. "No, go ahead." He wouldn't be going to sleep for a while yet anyway. "Would it bother you if I watched a little TV? I'll keep the volume down."

"Be my guest." With a shy smile, she ducked into the bathroom.

He stood there listening until he heard the lock click. Then he went into the living room and turned on the television. Unfortunately, the volume wasn't quite loud enough to drown out the sound of the shower. Visions of Alexandra wet and naked kept breaking his concentration, despite the fact that the police drama he was watching was one of his favorites. Time after time he lost the thread of the plot. Finally, he gave up and switched to a station showing *It's a Wonderful Life*. He'd seen the movie so many times, he knew most of the dialogue by heart. No need to pay attention. Instead, he indulged in a series of fantasies centered on Alexandra.

A prickle of unease assailed Alex as she stood in front of the mirror removing her makeup before entering the shower. Something was wrong. She spun around, searching the small bathroom for the source of her discomfort.

Her stomach gave a lurch when she finally realized what it was. The sliding shower door was open, one mirrored panel overlapping the other. Yet she knew she'd left them shut. She always left them shut.

Her heart beating out of control, Alex started to call Dixon, then remembered the preschooler who'd wiped his sticky fingers on one of the display quilts earlier that afternoon. As Alex had given the child and his mother the bum's rush out the front door, Mandy had hustled the quilt upstairs to soak the stains out in Alex's bathtub. No doubt she'd left the shower doors open when she was done.

Alex relaxed, relieved at the simple explanation. What was she so scared of anyway? She stuck her tongue out at her own pale reflection. She wasn't Janet Leigh and this wasn't *Psycho*.

She finished removing her makeup, then climbed into the shower, secure in the knowledge that her bodyguard was right outside the door. Her tense muscles relaxed under the soothing spray. She felt safe, really safe, for the first time in weeks. All thanks to Dixon Yano.

What might have happened if Dixon hadn't been keeping an eye on her at the party? She scrubbed her skin, trying to wash away the memory of Ed Loomis's hands.

Mark certainly hadn't been any help. If he hadn't conned her into rescuing Loomis from Tom, she'd have been spared the whole sordid episode—the whiskey breath, the clumsy pass, the nasty insinuations. What exactly had Loomis meant by saying what's sauce for the goose is sauce for the gander? She scrubbed even harder.

The problem with Mark was that he was so caught up in his own concerns, he didn't give her worries any serious consideration. He'd as much as said he thought she was imagining these attempts on her life. And as for his boss's repeated passes, Mark didn't seem to realize what was going on right under his nose. Just because his own motives were pure, he thought everyone else's were too.

Reluctantly, Alex turned off the spray. She wasn't really ready to leave the comforting warmth, but her fingers were becoming prunes. Besides, the hot-water heater had its limits and Dixon hadn't had his turn yet.

She slid the shower door open just far enough to snatch a couple of towels from the rack, then shut it quickly to hold in the steam. She wrapped her wet hair in one towel and dried herself with the other. Stepping out onto the mat, she shrugged into a terry-cloth robe and dropped the damp towel in the hamper.

Only when she slid the shower door shut did she notice the message scrawled in scarlet lipstick on the previously hidden half of the mirrored door: I'LL BE SEE-ING YOU.

Alex screamed. She couldn't help herself. She couldn't seem to stop, either.

Gradually she became aware of another noise, that of Dixon beating frantically at the locked door.

Her frightened screams died as abruptly as they'd begun.

"Open up, Alexandra! What's wrong? What's happened? Are you all right?"

Alex moved stiffly to the door and fumbled with the lock before she was able to release the catch.

Bursting into the room, Dixon seemed to take in both the intruder's message and Alex's precarious emotional state in one glance. He opened his arms and she fell against his chest.

"He was in here. He left a . . . message on . . . the mirror," she said jerkily, her words punctuated by painful sobs. She wasn't at all certain she was making sense. "I d-didn't see it until . . . I got out of the shower and slid the door shut."

"It's okay." He held her close, soothing her with

both his voice and his touch. "He can't hurt you now. I'm here."

Gradually, the warm comfort of his presence penetrated her distress. Her sobs lessened and, bit by bit, she regained a measure of control. Finally, embarrassed by her outburst and conscious of her reddened eyes and dripping nose, she detached herself. "I hope that sweater's washable." She sniffed. "I soaked it."

He passed her a handful of tissues from the box on the vanity.

"Thanks." She mopped at her eyes and blew her nose.

"Better?" He peered anxiously into her face.

She nodded and gave him a watery smile.

"You've had a lousy day, huh?"

She nodded again. "Should I call the police?" She didn't want to. All she wanted to do right now was go to sleep.

"Not tonight. Wait until morning. Unless you really want to spend all night answering questions."

She shook her head. No, she definitely didn't want that. What she wanted most of all right this minute was to be held securely in a pair of strong arms. She looked up into Dixon Yano's sad brown eyes. "Hold me?"

Without a word, he folded her against his chest. His sweater was scratchy against her cheek, but she could hear his heart beating fast and strong underneath, a comforting sound. They stood there for a long time, Dixon lending strength and comfort and she absorbing all he had to offer.

Alex wasn't sure when the new sensations began to creep in. At first she was aware only of comfort and reassurance emanating from his big, warm body. Then gradually, other, more dangerous sensations began to prickle at her nerve endings.

She wanted more than a reassuring hug. And it was obvious he did too.

But you're engaged, she reminded herself. To Mark.

When she pulled away, Dixon made no effort to hold her, just stuffed his hands into his back pockets as if he didn't know what else to do with them.

She couldn't quite meet his eyes. "I'm sorry." He surely knew what she meant. "I think I'd better go to my room now."

"Yes." His voice was rough, sandpaper to her exposed nerves. "That's a good idea."

She grabbed her comb and fled. But even after she had worked the snarls from her damp hair, she lay tossing and turning in bed, unable to sleep.

The past two days were a jumble of impressions replaying themselves over and over in her head. Dixon saying, "You don't look dead." Dixon bleeding after the rifle shot. Dixon running after the shooter before he got away. Dixon staring at her from across the room at her mother's party. Dixon doing his best to break Ed Loomis's jaw. Dixon holding her when she needed to be held.

Later, much later, she heard the shower running. Somehow she had a feeling she need not have worried about saving hot water.

"Oh, my God!" Alexandra's eyes grew round.

Dixon glanced at her reflection in the mirror and smiled through the lather on his face. "I hope you don't mind. I borrowed one of your razors." He waved a pink disposable.

"I . . . what are you doing here?"

"Shaving. Isn't it obvious?"

"But you're not dressed."

Dixon glanced down at his towel-clad hips. Careful not to disturb the lipsticked message on the mirrored door, he'd had a second shower this morning. Warm, this time. "I'm decent." He studied her shocked expression. Hadn't she ever seen a man in a towel before? "If it offends you, shut the door."

"You slept here last night?"

"Not here. In the bed—" His gaze narrowed. He spun around to confirm a sudden suspicion. Left eye blue. Right eye hazel. Not Alexandra. The sister, Mandy. Her mirrored image had confused him at first.

"Where's Alex?" Eyebrows lowered, she stared hard at him, as if she suspected foul play.

He shrugged. "She was already gone by the time I woke up."

"Does Mark know?"

"Does Mark know what?" asked Jordan, slipping up behind Mandy.

She jumped. "Where did *you* come from?"

"The front door was open, but I couldn't find anyone downstairs, so I came on up. Where's Alex?"

"I don't know. Ask him." She hooked a thumb in Dixon's direction.

"What the hell are you doing here?" Jordan sounded like the archetypal jealous fiancé, which Dixon found vaguely amusing considering the man's track record.

"Shaving."

"Before that."

"Showering."

"And before that?"

"Sleeping."

The lawyer made a sound deep in his throat, a cross between a growl and a gurgle. "And before that?"

Dixon tilted his head as if searching his memory, then let a satisfied smirk spread across his face. "Well, let's just say I didn't spend the *whole* night sleeping."

Jordan swore. "I don't know how the hell you wormed your way in here, but I want you out. Now."

Dixon wiped the last of the lather from his face. "Go suck an egg."

Jordan's fair skin turned beet red.

Dixon realized the man's intention almost before Jordan decided to act. Ducking a wild punch, Dixon swiveled on the balls of his feet, then doubled up Jordan with one hard jab to the solar plexus. He'd been aching to do that since the day before. Too bad his personal code forbade him kicking a man when he was down. Not that his bare feet would have inflicted much damage anyway.

In the background Mandy Sutton was saying "Oh, my God!" over and over.

"Oh, my God!" A new voice joined the chorus. "What's going on here?" It was Alexandra, her cheeks pink from the cold air outside. She clutched a white bakery sack in her gloved hands.

"That's what *I'd* like to know!" Jordan straightened up, one hand pressed to his stomach.

"Me too!" Mandy chimed in.

They both stared accusingly at Alexandra.

She glanced at Dixon, then back at the other two, then back at Dixon again. Their gazes locked and held.

"Nothing," he said, still watching Alexandra's eyes, still aware of her silent plea.

"The hell there's not!" Jordan had a lot of bluster left for someone who'd just had all the wind knocked out of him.

"Ms. Roundtree hired me as a bodyguard. Period. End of story."

"But before you made it sound—"

"Your attitude rubbed me the wrong way. You came in here making insinuations, demanding explanations. I just told you what you expected to hear."

Jordan turned to Alexandra. "Is that true? Nothing happened last night?"

Alexandra stiffened. She clutched the bakery sack so tightly, Dixon feared for his breakfast. "Other than Santa paying an early visit, you mean?"

"Santa?" Mandy echoed.

Alexandra ignored her sister. "Or are you referring to the police searching the premises for bombs, booby traps, and intruders?"

"None of which they found," Dixon added. "Though Santa did leave a memento." He slid the shower doors shut so the lipsticked message was visible.

" 'I'll be seeing you.' How creepy!" Mandy frowned. "Does that mean the psycho has you under surveillance?" She glanced over her shoulder as if searching for hidden cameras.

"Someone broke in last night while I was at the party, someone dressed in a Santa suit, probably the same someone who mugged me in the mall and took a potshot at me Wednesday afternoon in Dixon's office." Alexandra's voice shook. "When I got home last night, the back door was hanging open."

"Anything taken?"

Mandy's concern for her pocketbook was equal to, if not greater than, her concern for her sister's safety, Dixon thought cynically.

"Nothing I could see. We'll have to check stock against inventory to be sure."

"If you people will excuse me, I'd like to get dressed." Dixon twisted one corner of his mouth in a sardonic smile. "Of course, it's entirely up to you. I don't mind an audience." He put one hand on the towel as if he were about to let it drop.

Alexandra hustled the other two out and Dixon shut the door firmly behind the three of them.

"Personally, I wouldn't mind watching," he heard Mandy say, her voice only slightly muffled by the door. "The man has a gorgeous body. Are you sure—"

"Nothing happened," Alexandra snapped.

Dixon smiled to himself.

"So where'd everybody go?" Dixon asked, poking his head into the kitchen where Alexandra was shoveling coffee into a filter.

"To work. Where I should be."

"I thought the plan was for you to lie low for a while?"

"I'll go nuts if I spend another day cooped up in this apartment. Besides, Christmas is our busiest time of year. I can't leave Mandy and Shelby shorthanded." Her jaw was set. He could tell she wasn't going to change her mind in a hurry.

Alexandra pointed to the sack of assorted doughnuts from Sunrise Pastries. "Breakfast," she said. Shoving the basket into its slot, she threw the switch on her coffeemaker. "There's cereal in the cupboard if you'd prefer that. Eggs and juice in the refrigerator. Coffee'll be ready in a couple minutes." She refused to meet his gaze. Something else was bothering her.

"Did Jordan cool off?"

"Yes." She fiddled with the cuff of her red turtleneck. Her trousers were black-and-white houndstooth check today. She'd accessorized with lace-up boots and wide black suspenders that hugged the curve of her breasts. "No thanks to you. What did you tell him anyway?"

The corner of his mouth twitched. "I just said I didn't get much sleep last night. His nasty little mind filled in all the lurid details."

"There were no lurid details." She looked him straight in the eye.

"I know that."

"There aren't going to be any lurid details."

He made no comment.

Her chin came up. "I said, there aren't going to be any lurid details!"

"No need to shout. I heard you the first time."

"Then you should have acknowledged me."

"I said I heard you. I didn't say I agreed with you."

A fleeting emotion crossed her face, so fast that he had no time to identify it.

"I'm engaged." At the moment she didn't sound very happy about it.

Dixon sat at the little wooden dinette table and helped himself to a slightly mangled maple bar.

"I'm engaged to a wonderful man."

Yeah, a real peach of a guy. He ripped the maple bar in half, wishing it were Jordan's face.

"*Our* relationship is strictly business."

He met her gaze.

She flushed and looked away. "You're my body-guard," she told the vinyl flooring. "Just my bodyguard. Nothing else."

"That's what you're paying me for." He set the re-mains of his pastry on a napkin and crossed the small kitchen to her side.

"So long as we're agreed, then." She was still talking to the floor.

Dixon lifted her chin with gentle pressure from his index finger. "Look at me, Alexandra."

Reluctantly, she did. He had a feeling she was fight-ing herself as much as him.

"I would never do anything to hurt you. Do you believe that?"

"Yes." Her voice was a whisper.

"I will never take advantage of you. I will never do anything you don't want me to do. That's a promise. Okay?"

"Okay." She relaxed, her lovely smile shining with trust.

Dixon smiled back. "Shall we shake on it?"

She put her hand in his.

So small, he marveled. So delicate. Sometimes it was hard to believe men and women belonged to the same species.

They shook hands, then stood there for a moment, her hand warm in his. He watched the rapid rise and fall of her chest, the flutter of her eyelashes, the betraying color in her cheeks. A mistake, he thought. Touch trig-gered too many responses, both in her . . . and in him.

Drop her hand before you do something to screw this up, stupid!

"Thank you, Dixon." She twined her fingers through his, then brought his hand to her mouth and pressed a kiss on his knuckles.

She might as well have used a branding iron, he thought. Hope and despair battled in his head.

No matter what lies she told herself, he *knew* she was attracted to him. Just as he was attracted to her.

Remember what happened last time, the last shreds of his common sense reminded him. *It's Brittany all over again.*

He couldn't take much more of this. Her mouth was so close. All he had to do was bend a little closer to taste those soft red lips.

You're the professional here, bozo. So act like one. Gently, he disengaged his hand.

"You shouldn't have gone out alone this morning." He raised his hands to silence her automatic protest. "I know. Slipping out to the bakery wasn't a big risk, but it was still a risk. Until the police get this nut under lock and key, you need to be more careful."

She opened her mouth to say something, then closed it. She nodded. "You're right."

"Yeah." His smile was rueful. "That's what you pay me for."

FIVE

Dixon was on his forty-third game of computer solitaire. Fiddling around on the computer terminal in the partially enclosed office cubicle made it appear he was working, though actually, the customers were the focus of his attention. So far all he'd noticed was a little blue-haired lady who'd tried to rip off a couple of those overpriced crystal angels.

In one day he'd gone from licensed investigator to shoplifting patrol, not a smart career move. No doubt his mother would attribute the comedown to his unprofessional attire.

Shelby dropped a stack of invoices on the desk, then leaned over his shoulder, so close he could smell the mingled scents of her hairspray and her perfume. Paul Mitchell and Opium. Brittany's favorites. Dixon fought the urge to sneeze.

She leaned in closer so her breasts nudged his back and her hair tickled his ear. "Black jack on red queen," she suggested in a throaty whisper.

Dream on, Red. He'd been wary of redheads since carrot-topped Katie Meara had broken his heart back in third grade.

"Shelby!" Alexandra's voice was sharp. "Mrs. Bourasa is waiting for that estimate."

The redhead blew in his ear like some high-school seductress. "Later." She moved toward her impatient customer, employing a little more hip rotation than was strictly necessary.

Dixon found it a provocative and highly entertaining performance. He permitted himself a small smile.

"I'm paying you to watch out for possible attackers, not ogle the sales staff." Alexandra's outraged whisper sounded right in his ear. She'd taken up Shelby's former position near his shoulder.

Jealous? He clicked the mouse to dump the jack of spades on the queen of hearts, then glanced sideways at her. "What makes you think Cousin Shelby's not the would-be killer?"

Alexandra rolled her eyes. "She has no motive."

"Don't be so sure. It could be a twisted *Fatal Attraction* thing. Maybe she wants you out of the way so she can have Jordan all to herself."

Alexandra gave an unladylike snort of laughter. "No chance. Mark and Shelby can't stand each other. When I first started going with Mark, Shel did her best to turn me against him. And he avoids *her* like the plague." She shrugged. "Negative chemistry, I guess."

Or a damned good cover-up. Dixon swiveled around in his chair to face her directly. "So tell me, Alexandra, who does have a motive? Who stands to gain from your death?"

Every trace of amusement disappeared from her face.

"Just Mandy and my mother. If I die, Mandy gets my half of the business plus a quarter of my trust fund. Everything else goes to my mother." She paused. "But I can't believe . . . neither Mother nor Mandy would . . . no, it's crazy!"

"Either of them having cash-flow problems?"

She bit her lip. "I know Mother was disappointed with her last royalty check, and she did spend more than anticipated on the new house. . . ."

"And your sister?"

"Tom and Mandy are well-off. Okay, they have sunk a bundle in Tom's clinic, and I know things are a little tight right now, but . . ." She looked troubled.

"How about your fiancé?"

"Mark wants to marry me, not kill me." She spoke emphatically, but she didn't look at him.

Dixon suspected Alexandra wasn't as sure of Jordan's loyalty as she was trying to pretend. "The question is, would he benefit financially from your death?"

"No. I told you. Mandy and my mother inherit everything."

"Everything?"

She bit her lip. "Almost everything. Mark *is* the beneficiary of my life insurance."

"How much?"

"A hundred thousand."

Dixon gave a long, low whistle of surprise. A hundred thou?

Alexandra's jaw tightened. "Don't look that way. Mark's no threat. His insurance names me beneficiary too. Does that automatically make me a murder suspect?"

"Jordan's not the one who's been having 'accidents.' "

She shifted her gaze to stare out across the cluttered shop, seemingly fascinated by the pile of red-and-green wicker baskets her sister was showing some customers.

Shelby ushered Mrs. Bourasa out the front door, then trotted quickly back to the office. "Mind if I take off for lunch a little early? I ripped a fingernail assembling one of those wretched bent-willow crèches." She waved her cherry-red talons under Alexandra's nose. The nail on her right index finger had a minuscule nick. "My manicurist said she'd try to squeeze me in if I can get there before twelve-thirty."

Alexandra nodded. "Sure, go ahead."

Dixon waited until Shelby was out of earshot, then resumed his questioning. "All right, think, Alexandra. Aside from those who stand to profit from your death, do you have any enemies?"

She chewed her lip. "Not really. There is a checker at Albertson's with an attitude. I try to avoid her because she always manages to crush my eggs and smash my bread. I'm sure she does it on purpose, but I don't have a clue why."

"She hates you because you're beautiful?"

"That motivation only works in fairy tales." Gnawing at her lip some more, she frowned.

"An old boyfriend?" he suggested. "A disgruntled former employee? A dissatisfied customer?"

"Danny Hall." She spoke slowly. "I'd almost forgotten about him."

From the look on her face, Dixon wished he hadn't had to remind her. "A former boyfriend?"

"No." She shook her head emphatically. "Never. No

way. He *repulses* me." She shuddered at the thought. "Hall used to live with Julie Yeager, one of our employees. He knocked her around on a regular basis. Julie finally kicked him out, but he refused to leave her alone. The situation got very nasty. Threats and restraining orders. One night he forced his way into Julie's place and beat the daylights out of her." She sighed. "He ended up doing jail time. Since I was the one who turned him in, I suppose he might be carrying a grudge." She looked doubtful. "All that happened over three years ago, though."

"No other enemies?"

"Not really."

She was lying. She couldn't even look him in the eye. "You're holding out on me, Alexandra."

It was a wonder her lip wasn't hamburger the way she kept chewing on it. "Well, there *is* one more possibility."

"Who?"

"Mark's ex-wife, Colleen."

"What about her?"

"She called me one day, shortly after the announcement of my engagement appeared in the paper."

"And?"

"Mark had warned me about her."

I just bet he did.

"She's a very disturbed woman."

Dixon held his tongue. He couldn't very well spill his guts without checking first with his former client.

"She made all kinds of crazy claims."

"Such as?"

"Such as Mark was a philanderer. 'President of the Society of Cheating Husbands,' as she put it. Pretty far-fetched considering she was the one who had a lover on the side."

"Mark told you that?"

She nodded. "Oh, he didn't want to admit it, but he thought I ought to be warned just in case she tried to poison my mind against him—which, of course, is exactly what she did." She wrinkled her nose. "She was very believable too." Alexandra fell silent, her face reflecting inner turmoil.

"You suspect at least part of what she told you was true."

Her gaze met his. She looked miserable. "I don't know what's true anymore. Mark says she's dangerous, but . . ." She shrugged, then shook her head. "Even if she is bitter over the divorce, that's still no motive to get rid of me. Unless she's completely irrational, she must know Mark would never take her back, not after the way she hurt him."

I'd like to hurt that lying son of a bitch. Again.

He glanced up as the bells above the front door jangled, a wave of pure rage washing over him when he saw who the customer was. Mark Jordan strolled up the center aisle, a complacent smile on his handsome face.

Jordan's attention was focused on his fiancée, but Dixon noticed the way the two customers talking to Mandy, both women, followed Jordan's progress. What did females find so damn charismatic about the scrawny blond creep, anyway? he wondered.

"Ready for lunch, darling?" Jordan asked.

"Anytime you are, sweetheart," Dixon replied, standing and reaching for his jacket.

A frown wrinkled Jordan's forehead and tightened the corners of his mouth. "Very funny, Yano. I wasn't talking to you." He turned to Alexandra. "How about it, Alex? There's a turkey-and-cheddar croissant out there with your name on it."

"I . . ." She glanced at Dixon. "We do need to talk, but—"

"But what? I think the shop can get along without you for an hour."

"No, that's not it." She frowned. "It's just that I can't go anywhere without Dixon."

Dixon fought the urge to jump on the counter, pound his chest, and let loose with a Tarzan yell. "It's part of the job description," he explained to Jordan. "A bodyguard has to stay in close proximity to the body he's guarding."

Jordan said a very rude word under his breath. "I think Alex is safe enough with me."

Dixon shrugged into his jacket. "Why don't we let Alexandra be the judge of that?"

"Alex?" Raising one eyebrow, Jordan crossed his arms over his chest.

"I hired Dixon to protect me. It doesn't make any sense not to let him do the job he's being paid to do, does it?"

"No, I suppose not." Jordan's capitulation was grudging.

"That's settled, then. I'll go get my coat." She whisked away up the stairs.

Jordan glared at him. "You're a real piece of work, Yano. You might have Alex fooled, but don't think I don't know what you're after."

"What's that?" Dixon's tone was deceptively mild.

"The beautiful heiress." He spat the words out. "You think all you have to do is shake the money tree and Alex'll drop into your lap like a windfall. Well, forget it.

I've invested a lot of time and effort in her, and I don't intend to bow out gracefully—not until I've collected the grand prize."

Dixon cocked his head to the side. "The grand prize?"

"Two million dollars in trust until she turns thirty or gets married, whichever comes first."

Dixon sucked air for a second or two. She'd mentioned a trust fund, but he'd had no idea the Roundtrees had that kind of money.

Another thought occurred to him. Damn. Much as he'd like to pin the murder attempts on Jordan, that scenario now seemed highly unlikely. The jerk had means and opportunity, but no motive. What was a hundred thou in insurance compared with two million in trust-fund dollars? Double damn. Apparently the guy wasn't murdering scum, just scum.

"I've got your number, too, Jordan. In case you haven't figured it out already, I'm the one who gathered all the evidence your ex-wife used to ream your ass in court. Push me too far and I'll tell Alexandra what I know."

"Go ahead." Mark Jordan's smile was distinctly unpleasant. "She won't believe you. She loves me."

They walked three abreast across the street to Sandy's Sandwich Shoppe, the men flanking Alex. She shivered in her bulky down-filled coat. The sky was a clear robin's-egg blue, but though the sun shone brightly, it gave off precious little warmth. A sharp wind rattled the halos on the tacky plastic angels that hung from every streetlight on Oregon Street and fluttered the fairy lights Sandy'd strung along the naked branches of the Japanese maple that shaded her stretch of sidewalk in summer. Down at the end of the block a skinny Santa hugged himself against the cold, rocking back and forth in time with the bell he rang over a Salvation Army kettle.

Alex smiled teasingly up at Dixon as they entered the warmth of Sandy's shop. "I can't believe you've never eaten here before. Your office is only four blocks away. What do you do for lunch?"

"Brown-bag it most of the time. Once in a while I splurge on pizza or a Big Mac."

"A true gourmet." Mark's smile was almost a sneer.

He and Dixon didn't seem to like each other much, Alexandra couldn't help noticing. No doubt it was a man thing.

"What are you wearing tonight?" Mark posed the question as soon as they had placed their orders and seated themselves at a table in the back of the long, narrow lunchroom.

Alex shot him a questioning glance before taking a sip of her diet soda. "What's tonight?"

"Don't tell me you've forgotten. We planned this weeks ago."

Alex stared at him blankly. Weeks ago. Before some nutcase in a Santa suit entered her life. "Refresh my memory."

"Cocktail party at the Loomises'. Ed's going to announce the new partner. God, Alex. How could you forget something like that?"

Dixon grunted. "She's had other things on her mind."

Mildly irritated at his presumption, Alex placed a restraining hand on his arm. "I do have a tongue, you know. I'm perfectly capable of speaking for myself."

Dixon made a cross with his index fingers and held it out in front of him as if warding off evil spirits.

She smiled at his foolishness. "Idiot."

"Second that motion," Mark snapped.

She turned to him, her smile disappearing. "As Dixon said, I've had other things on my mind. Someone is trying to kill me, Mark, and the scary part is, they're not even bothering to make it look like an accident anymore."

"Darling, I know you've been under a lot of stress. But this is important. My career—"

"Your career?" Her voice rose shrilly. "How does your career compare to my life?"

Dixon gave her arm a warning squeeze as some of the luncheon crowd turned to stare.

Mark frowned. "Keep your voice down. People know me here."

Alex couldn't believe what she was hearing. "Mark, listen to yourself. You're more worried about your image than about the fact that your fiancée's in danger. Don't you care that someone's trying to kill me?"

"Alex, I love you dearly. You know that. If anything happened to you, I couldn't bear it."

Dixon's fingers tightened again on her arm.

"But?" Somehow she knew there was a but. With lawyers, there always was.

"But I'm not convinced your life is in danger."

She stiffened in outrage. "You think I made it all up?"

"No," he said hastily. "I'm merely suggesting that you've misinterpreted certain events."

He didn't believe a word she'd said. Her cheeks stung as if he'd slapped her. "For example?"

"Okay, someone has threatened you. I have no argument with that. What I don't necessarily buy is that this mysterious someone is trying to kill you. Neither the short in the Christmas lights on the store display nor the collapsing float was a surefire method to murder someone. I think the 'accidents,' like the anonymous note and the lipsticked message on the shower door, were warnings, not actual attempts on your life."

Alex frowned. "What about the mugging?"

Mark shrugged. "An act of random violence"—he held up a hand to forestall her objections—"or a clever way to get your keys. In my opinion, the shove down the stairs was more a matter of expediency than a deliberate attempt to harm you."

Alexandra was so angry she was shaking. "Two days ago someone shot at me. Explain that away."

"Like I said before, the bullet could have been meant for Yano, not you."

"You're wrong—"

"Maybe." He cut her off smoothly, his voice determinedly reasonable.

"Dammit, Mark. Are you suggesting I'm delusional?"

He smiled and patted her hand. "No, but I think you're too close to the action to view matters objectively. Paranoia has set in, Alex, and no wonder. If I'd grown up in the same house with the reigning queen of the mystery genre, I'd probably see criminal intent in ordinary, everyday events myself."

Since when was being shot at an ordinary, everyday event for anyone besides James Bond? she wondered, shooting a quick glance toward Dixon. His jaw was clenched, his expression thunderous. He, at least, took her fears seriously.

One of the waitresses brought their orders then, so Alex swallowed the protest she'd been about to make. She hoped it wouldn't give her indigestion.

Seemingly oblivious to her anger, Mark tasted his soup, then sighed in satisfaction. "Best chowder in town."

"Here. Have mine." Dixon tipped his bowl into Mark's lap.

Stifling a curse, Mark leaped to his feet as the scalding liquid soaked through his trousers.

Dixon's gaze was limpidly innocent. "Oops. Sorry, buddy. I guess I slipped."

"You son of a bitch!"

"Careful, Jordan. People know you here. You don't want to give them the wrong impression."

Alex fought to keep from laughing at the outraged expression on Mark's face.

"Excuse me," he said stiffly, and moved off toward the men's room, walking rather oddly.

"That was a rotten thing to do," Alexandra said to Dixon as soon as Jordan was out of earshot.

Dixon grinned. "It was an accident." He shrugged and took a bite of his sandwich. "Just as much an accident as the 'ordinary, everyday events' you're so 'paranoid' about."

"It's rude to talk with your mouth full."

"It's rude to talk with your brain empty, but that doesn't seem to stop your fiancé. What do you see in that jerk?"

Alex was beginning to wonder. Instead of answering, she took a bite of her sandwich. Dammit. Right now she needed Mark's support, not specious reasoning or a condescending "understanding" of her so-called psychological problems. She was worried, yes. Scared too. But not paranoid.

Was Mark really that insensitive? Or did his stubborn refusal to take the threats seriously stem from a more sinister motive? What if Mark himself had orchestrated the accidents?

She swallowed hard and glanced up to find Dixon staring at her. "What? Do I have mustard on my nose?"

He shook his head. "No, I was just thinking about this party tonight. Maybe we should go."

"You're joking. After the Loomis fiasco last night?"

"Trust me. Loomis won't pull anything with me sticking to you like a cocklebur. I'm assuming this will be a big party?"

She nodded. "Everyone connected with the firm plus all their top-drawer clients and the local bigwigs."

"Your mother?"

"Definitely."

"How about your sister and her husband?"

"Yes, they're on the A-list too. So?"

He leaned his chin against his steepled fingers. "So it means we'd have most of the known suspects together in one place, a situation which offers some intriguing investigative possibilities. And you should be safe enough in a crowd as long as you steer clear of any poisoned eggnog."

"No problem." Alexandra made a face. "I hate eggnog."

"Or we play it safe and stay in the apartment." Dixon shrugged. "Your choice."

Alex sighed. "Even in the apartment there are no

guarantees of my safety. Santa got in last night while I was gone. Who's to say he won't come back tonight?"

Dixon looked grim. "If he does, I'll be ready for him."

"Excuse me? Ms. Roundtree?" The waitress hovered at her elbow.

"Yes?"

"Mr. Jordan gave me a note for you." She laid a folded paper towel on the blue-checked tablecloth next to Alex's plate.

"Thanks." Wondering what Mark was up to, Alexandra smiled an acknowledgment at the girl. Now what? Had the office beeped him? Sometimes she suspected he was more closely engaged to the firm than to her. She unfolded the towel and read in silence.

After a long pause Dixon cleared his throat. "What is it?"

She made a face. "He couldn't remove the stain from his trousers, so he slipped out the back to avoid notice. He's rushing home to change before his one o'clock appointment."

Dixon's grin made him look like an ornery ten-year-old.

"There's a message for you too," Alexandra continued. "Interested?"

"You bet."

"Mark says the party tonight is formal, and if you don't have a tux, you can't go. Bodyguard or no bodyguard."

"Are we planning to attend, then?"

She nodded, making up her mind. If she sat around waiting for Santa to make his next move, she'd go crazy. "Don't worry about a tux. The woman who owns the bridal shop next door is an old friend. She'll give me a discount."

"Not a problem. I have a monkey suit, a relic of my sister's wedding."

"Good. It's settled, then."

Dixon kept her distracted throughout the rest of the meal with a series of truly awful knock-knock jokes. She was still groaning as they emerged from the deli to the bitter chill outside. "Your sense of humor is seriously warped."

Afterward, she wasn't certain exactly what happened next. One minute she was standing on the curb, laughing up at Dixon, and the next she was lying prone in the street, watching a car bearing down on her.

"Catch that Santa!" she heard Dixon yell. Then Dixon's strong arms were pulling her to safety.

Alex clung to him. She hurt all over, her palms, her elbows, and most of all her knees. "What happened? Did I slip on the ice?"

Dixon's face was dark with anger, but she knew his rage wasn't directed toward her. His hands cradled her gently; his voice soothed. "You were pushed. Our old friend Santa Claus again. I'm afraid he got away. By the time I'd pulled you back to the sidewalk . . ."

She struggled to a sitting position. "I guess it's time to call the cops again, huh?"

He nodded grimly. "Already taken care of."

Dixon was getting sick of repeating himself. "Like I already told you twice, Cesar, all I saw was somebody in a Santa suit." He frowned. "How come you responded to the call, anyhow? I thought you were working swing."

Cesar washed down his second hunk of fudge with a swig of coffee.

Dixon suspected his friend had an ulterior motive for conducting this interview in the break room of Gemini Gifts. Officer Rios's sweet tooth was legendary.

Cesar reached for a third piece of fudge. "I'm pulling a double shift today. Harrison and Echanis are both out with flu." He refilled his mug, added three sugars, and stirred vigorously. "When I spoke with Ms. Roundtree earlier, she mentioned seeing a Salvation Army Santa ringing a bell on the corner as she entered the sandwich shop. Are you sure you didn't notice him?"

"I've already answered this question. Twice. Here's number three: No, Officer Rios, I didn't notice the Salvation Army Santa. I wish I had, but I didn't."

"Weird, huh? You'd think a bell-ringing guy in a red suit would stick out like a sore thumb."

"Look, Cesar, maybe if it were the middle of July, he would have. But the fact is, Santas are a dime a dozen during the Christmas season. I admit I should have noticed. Normally I would have noticed. But today I was distracted."

"Distracted?" Cesar smirked. He knew damn well what Dixon meant.

"By Ms. Roundtree."

Cesar laughed. "Just wanted to hear you admit it, man. Never thought I'd see the day you'd let another female penetrate your armor." He downed his coffee in a few quick gulps. "They're not all like Brittany, you know. In fact, damn few of them are."

"She's engaged, Cesar."

"Brittany? Didn't know you'd kept in touch." A fourth chunk of homemade fudge disappeared.

"No, not Brittany. I haven't thought of her in years." Which was a damn lie. He thought of her every time he used a credit card.

"You mean Ms. Roundtree's engaged? No wonder you're in such a stinking mood, man. That really throws a kink in your rope."

"Are we finished?" Dixon stood. The break-room walls were starting to close in on him.

"What's your hurry?" Cesar picked a fudge crumb from a wrinkle of his blue uniform shirt. "Who's the lucky fiancé?"

"Mark Jordan. Do you know him?"

"I've seen him. He's a lawyer, right?"

"Right. Tollman, Loomis, and Taylor."

"Blond guy? Looks like he ought to be modeling underwear in the Penney's catalog?"

"Yeah, that's Jordan."

Cesar grunted. "Poor slob doesn't stand a chance." He raised an eyebrow. "Neither do you, man. I've seen the way you look at her." He grinned. "And the way she looks back."

SIX

"This is a crock, Alexandra. No way should you be going to Loomis's party." Dixon frowned and tugged at his tie. He'd forgotten how uncomfortable the tux was. He felt like he was choking to death.

Alexandra's eyebrows rose. "I don't look that bad, do I?"

"No." She looked gorgeous in a snug-fitting red dress, but it didn't require the intuition of Sherlock Holmes to realize she wasn't feeling up to par. He'd watched her downing aspirin like candy all afternoon. And he knew about the scrapes and bruises hidden beneath her long sleeves and flowing skirt. She was wearing more makeup than normal too. Dixon suspected she needed the extra color to disguise the unhealthy pallor of her cheeks.

A teasing smile lit her face. "You're being deliberately dense, aren't you? I was fishing for a compliment. You were supposed to tell me that no, of course, I don't look that bad. On the contrary, you were supposed to say, I look fabulous"—she batted her lashes—"stunning"—she modulated her voice to a husky whisper—"ravishing."

The corner of his mouth twitched. "What you said."

Alexandra put one hand to her heart. "Flatterer."

Playing along, Dixon struck a pose, one hand gripping his lapel, the other resting on the mantel. "Your turn."

Alexandra tipped her head to one side, studying him. Her smile made his heartbeat accelerate alarmingly. "Oh, Dixon." She bit her lower lip. "You look like you're in imminent danger of strangling to death." Her throaty chuckle sent a shiver down his spine. "Here. Let me fix that tie."

She positioned herself in front of him, so close it was all he could do not to pull her into his arms.

His cognitive processes slowed to a crawl. Thoughts of Alexandra filled his mind. Alexandra—so lovely, so feminine, so . . . engaged.

Reaching up, she deftly retied his tie, much more loosely this time, though he still was having some trouble breathing.

"Thanks." His voice was hoarse.

She smoothed his lapels, then ran her fingertips lightly across his cheek. "I see you shaved again."

He swallowed hard. "Had to. I develop five o'clock shadow around noon." *That's it. Keep it light, Yano. Try not to think about the fact that those facial nerves she just touched seem to be directly connected to your crotch.*

She smiled approvingly. "You look like a Hollywood hunk. You'll have every woman in the place throwing herself at you."

Every woman except the one woman he cared about.

He cleared his throat and asked gruffly, "How are your knees?"

She pulled up the hem of her skirt. The bandages were clearly visible through the thin nylon of her panty hose. "Fine as long as I don't bend them. If you notice me walking like a robot, you'll know why." She let her skirt drop and glanced up at him. "I'm not complaining, you understand. If it weren't for your quick thinking, I'd be in worse shape. Did I thank you yet for saving my life?"

"No need. That's what you're paying me for." *Don't look at me that way, Ms. Roundtree. If you don't knock it off, I'm going to have to kiss you.*

"Yes need." Alexandra stood on tiptoe, wrapped both arms around his neck, and gently pressed her lips to his.

The hallucination was so vivid, Dixon could swear he felt the softness of her mouth against his own.

"Thank you." She whispered the words, her breath caressing his lips.

Not a hallucination. Reality. Jeez.

The doorbell rang before he could take advantage of the situation.

Alexandra stepped back, casually glancing down at her watch. "That must be Mark. On time as usual." She smiled. "Wait till he hears what you did. He'll want to thank you too."

Dixon raised an eyebrow. "Okay, but no kissing. I'm not that kind of guy."

Alex ducked into the Loomises' powder room, sank down on the ivory brocade love seat just inside the door, and buried her head in her hands. Her temples throbbed with every beat of her heart. Dixon had been right. She really wasn't up to this.

"Having fun, dear?" Regina emerged from behind the partition that hid the toilet. She washed her hands, then paused in front of the mirror to adjust her hat, an outrageous sequined cloche trimmed with curling ostrich feathers.

Alex didn't say a word, just sent her mother a bleak look that spoke volumes.

"What's wrong? Are you and Mark fighting? I noticed he's spent the entire evening sucking up to the host and hostess while virtually ignoring you."

Alex shook her head. "No, it's this killer headache. I shouldn't have come."

"You do look pale. Dixon told me about your close call this afternoon." Regina sat next to Alex, wrapping a comforting silk-clad arm around her shoulders.

"I'm scared, Mother. If Dixon hadn't been there to pull me back to safety . . ." She shuddered.

"Alex, I don't think you should stay in the apartment any longer. Or even in Brunswick. Why don't you and your bodyguard fly to Maui for a week? I'd be happy to pick up the tab."

"Let me see. A week in paradise with another man? Yes, I'm sure Mark would go for that. Get real, Mother."

"Then hide out in Cleveland. Or Salt Lake. Or Timbuktu. I don't care where you go as long as you put some distance between yourself and whoever's after you."

Alex sighed. "Dixon agrees, but this is our busiest time at the shop. If I left Mandy in the lurch, I wouldn't have to worry about a mystery assailant; she'd kill me herself."

"Then move in with me for a while."

"I'll think about it," Alex promised. She stood. "Right now, though, I'm going to find Dixon and have him take me home."

Regina rose in one lithe movement and gave Alex a quick hug. "Sounds like a plan, baby."

Unfortunately, finding Dixon proved to be easier said than done. He wasn't in the dining room among the crowd circling the hors d'oeuvres like vultures. Nobody'd seen him in the media room, and the sunroom was empty. Reluctantly, she headed for the family room, where Ed Loomis was holding court.

She slipped inside and, positioning herself behind a lush ficus, scanned the interior. Dixon caught her gaze from across the room. "Where have you been?" she mouthed.

Frowning slightly and shaking his head from side to side, he maneuvered his way through the crowd. "Scouring the house searching for you. I was afraid you'd had another run-in with your unfriendly neighborhood Santa. Where *were* you, Alexandra?"

"Powder room."

"Are you feeling all right? You look tired."

"I have a headache," she admitted.

His frown was an accusation.

"Yes, I know. I shouldn't have come. You were right. I should have listened."

"Yes, you should have." His expression was grim. "I'll take you home."

"Not so fast. I have to say good-bye to Mark first."

"Well, he's not in the living room. I just came from there."

"He's not in the dining room, media room, or sun-room, either."

"Maybe he left already."

She shook her head. "Not before the new partner-ship's announced."

Dixon scanned the crowd. "So where is he?"

"The library maybe?" She shrugged.

"Shall we?" Dixon held out his arm.

Alex balked. Yes, she was paying him to keep her safe, but that didn't mean he had to follow her everywhere—especially not into Mark's vicinity. After the soup inci-dent that afternoon and the wrangling over who drove earlier that evening, she doubted Mark would be exactly thrilled to run into Dixon again. Her head hurt enough already. She didn't feel up to playing referee for a couple of squabbling males. "No need for you to trouble your-self. I'll only be a second."

Dixon gripped her upper arms. "Look, Alexandra."

She smiled up at him expectantly. She loved the way he said her name.

Dixon swallowed hard. An odd, almost flustered ex-pression crossed his rugged face. "Look, I've been going crazy for the last half hour, wondering where you'd dis-appeared to. I'm not about to let you out of my sight a second time. How do you expect me to do my job if you won't cooperate?"

He wasn't going to give in. She could read determi-nation in the stubborn line of his jaw. "All right, but if you pick another fight with Mark—"

"I won't." Releasing her, he crossed his heart. "I'll be on my best behavior. Promise."

She didn't believe him for a second, but she couldn't

resist the entreaty in his smile. "Okay. Come on. The sooner we find Mark, the sooner we can leave." She led the way up the stairs, her abraded knees protesting at each step.

For the third time in under an hour the Bing Crosby version of "White Christmas" blared through the stereo system. Alex suspected the song was not only Eileen's favorite, but also the theme of her decor.

The big neo-Victorian house had been decorated—overdecorated in Alex's opinion—in stark white. Flocked pine garlands trimmed with oversized satin bows hung in swags along the stair railing. Huge snowy-white artificial trees, drooping under a load of pearly beads, satin balls, and crocheted angels, dominated the entry hall, living room, and family room. Thousands of lace snowflakes hung suspended around the house. It was enough to induce snow blindness.

"All the warmth and charm of a meat locker," Dixon muttered.

"Or an igloo."

Dixon paused at the top of the stairs. "Where's the library?"

"First door on the left." She turned to face him. "Wait here?" It was more request than order.

He nodded.

Alex slipped inside the long, narrow room that doubled as Ed Loomis's home office. Despite the way she felt about Loomis, his library was, oddly enough, her favorite spot in the house. She loved the odor of leather upholstery mingling with the faint mildewy scent of old books.

Here the sterile white had given way to rich burgundy and teal, a feast for her color-starved eyes. She coveted the jewel-toned carpet, and although the heavy mahogany furniture was too ornate for her taste, its bulk was perfectly proportioned for the spacious, high-ceilinged room.

At first glance she thought the library was empty. Then she noticed the couple standing motionless near the stained-glass window, locked in a passionate embrace.

Her heart hammered madly. She felt faint. Quietly, she ducked back out.

"Alexandra, what is it?" Dixon must have read something in her expression.

She shook her head and headed for the stairs. "Nothing. Let's go."

"What about Mark? Did you talk to him?"

She gave another jerky little shake of her head. "No. He was busy."

"Too busy for his fiancée?"

Much too busy. He'd had his mouth glued to his hostess's collagen-enhanced lips. Eileen Loomis was an attractive woman in a brittle sort of way, but she was also considerably closer to Regina's age than Alex's. Was Mark that desperate for a promotion?

"Alexandra?" Dixon sounded worried.

"Let's go," she said. She suspected her face was as pale and bloodless as Eileen Loomis's decor.

Dixon gripped her forearm, halting her headlong flight down the broad staircase. "Alexandra, talk to me."

She couldn't talk to him. Not about this. "I'm tired, Dixon. Please take me home."

He didn't argue. She liked that about him.

Outside, the temperature had dropped at least twenty

degrees, but Alex scarcely felt the cold. She was too numb to feel much of anything.

The sky overhead was full of stars. A line from an old carol ran through her head. *It came upon a midnight clear.* A joyful message or a devastating one—depending entirely on what "it" was. The diamond set in her engagement ring echoed the cold sparkle of the faraway stars. She turned the stone toward her palm so she wouldn't have to look at it.

Something was bothering Alexandra, something more than a headache. Dixon parked the Jeep behind the store, turned the engine off, and doused the lights. She just sat there in the passenger's seat, making no move to get out.

He touched her hand. It was icy. "You're home, Alexandra."

She moved then, jerkily, as if he'd startled her out of a daydream. "Dixon?"

"You're home," he repeated. "You'd better come inside before you freeze to death."

Tonight the parking area behind the stores was nearly deserted, the only other vehicles Alexandra's black Stealth and the van that belonged to the furniture store at the other end of the block. He wondered idly where bums like Myron holed up on nights like these. Someplace warm, he hoped.

The spicy scent of potpourri enveloped him as he pushed open the back door to the shop. The fragrance reminded him of the Christmases of his childhood, of his mother's krumkake and the special Swedish tea ring she always prepared for the holidays.

He ushered Alexandra inside and locked the door securely behind them. The shiny new dead bolt she'd had installed first thing that morning was a great improvement over the old lock.

He glanced down at his watch, surprised to discover how early it was. "How's your head?"

"Fine." A frown knit her brow.

Liar, he thought. "Are you hungry?"

"Not really, but I'll cook something if you'd like." She turned toward the stairs.

"Don't bother." He followed her up the steps, talking to her back. "I'm used to taking care of myself. I may not be much good in the kitchen, but I can order a mean pizza."

She flicked on the lights then moved across the room to the window, where she stood staring moodily down at the street. "Dixon?"

"What?" He'd been flipping through the Yellow Pages in search of the number for the local pizza place, but he laid the phone directory aside at the look on her face. "What is it?" He crossed the room in three strides.

Her eyes were glassy with unshed tears.

Dixon led her to the sofa, where they sat, thighs touching, hands entwined. "What's wrong, Alexandra?"

She dropped her gaze, staring fixedly at his right lapel. "Have you ever been in love, Dixon?"

"I thought I was once."

"Me too." She looked up at him, and her eyes brimmed over.

He gathered her into his arms, moving cautiously, half-afraid she'd rebuff his attempt to comfort her, but she melted against him, wrapping her arms around his neck.

"It's okay," he whispered against her hair. "It's okay," though he knew it wasn't.

She was warm as sunshine, soft as silk. And her scent . . . her scent was as sweetly intoxicating as the fragrance of roses on a hot summer day. Closing his eyes, Dixon let his hands slide down the curve of her back. He buried his face in her hair, drugging himself in the scents and textures of her. Since the first moment he'd laid eyes on Alexandra Roundtree, he'd wanted to do this. This and more.

Only she's engaged to another man, he reminded himself. Gently he loosened her hands and sat back so he could study her face. "What happened?"

Her lower lip quivered. "Mark was in the library with Eileen Loomis . . . kissing her." She shuddered. "I couldn't believe it. I still can't. It's a nightmare."

Dixon tilted her chin up with his forefinger. "Facing up to unwelcome truths is never much fun, but maybe it's for the best."

"The best?" She caught her breath on a sob.

He opened his mouth to tell her about the evidence he'd gathered for Colleen Jordan, then changed his mind. It wasn't his place to divulge that information.

"Well?"

He couldn't betray client confidentiality, but those rules didn't apply to everything he knew. "Isn't it better to discover what kind of man Jordan is now—before you're married?"

She shook her head. "I don't know. I keep thinking I must have misunderstood what I saw." She shook her head. "Mark wouldn't have . . . he's not like that."

Dixon gathered her hands in his. "I think he's exactly like that."

"Meaning?" The trembling of her fingers telegraphed the degree of her anxiety.

He gave her hands a comforting squeeze. How do you tell someone they're engaged to a scumbag, especially when you know that's not the story they want to hear? "Last night when I went up to get your coat . . ."

"Yes?"

"The bedroom door was locked."

"Mark and Eileen? They were together in my mother's bedroom?" A strange emotion quivered across Alexandra's face. She looked so vulnerable, so devastated, Dixon wished he'd kept his mouth shut. "So that's what Loomis was talking about." Her voice cracked on the last word.

"No," he said. He didn't want her jumping to conclusions, but damn, he didn't want to tell her the truth either.

"No?" A faint ray of hope glimmered in her eyes.

Dixon hated to quench that light. "No," he repeated. "I saw only Mark."

"But if he was alone, why was the door locked?"

"Good question. He said the lock on the bathroom door was messed up and he didn't want anyone walking in on him."

Alexandra studied their entwined fingers. "Mother's only lived in that house for two months. I can't believe there's anything wrong with the lock." She looked up at Dixon. "You suspect he'd been making love with someone, someone who was hiding in the bathroom."

"The thought crossed my mind," he admitted, "as soon as I saw the earring on the bed."

"An earring?"

"It had slid down between the pillows as if—"

She cut him off. "How did Mark explain the earring?" Her nails dug into his hands.

"He said your mother probably dropped it."

"It *is* her room." She frowned. "What kind of earring was it?"

He shrugged. "It looked like a Christmas ornament."

"No, I mean was it for pierced or unpierced ears?"

"I don't know. What's the difference? It had a little hook on it, I think, just like a real Christmas ornament."

"Pierced," she said. "It wasn't my mother's, then." She squeezed his hands in a desperate grip, as if he were her lifeline to sanity. "So it could have been Eileen skulking in the bathroom."

"It could have been, I guess."

She looked up sharply. "But you don't think so. Why?"

"Because I saw someone earlier in the evening wearing an identical pair of earrings."

"Who?" Alexandra's mouth formed the word, though no sound emerged from her throat.

"Your cousin Shelby."

Dixon lay in bed, staring at the ceiling. He couldn't sleep. He kept remembering the scene in the living room, the scents and textures of Alexandra's body as vivid in his memory as her words.

Another sort of man, a brighter man, would have taken advantage of her vulnerability. But then, if he were a brighter man, he would have married some nice girl right out of college instead of getting involved with a soulless bitch like Brittany Farrell. And no two ways about it, a brighter man, having survived such a damag-

ing encounter, would have been forever immune to the
seductiveness of a beautiful face.

Yet here he was, obsessed with Alexandra Roundtree.

Alex paced the apartment, unable to sleep. Every
time she closed her eyes she remembered the cold, incredulous shock of the moment she'd first seen Mark and
Eileen in the library. His hands, the same hands that had
held her so lovingly, wrapped around Eileen. His mouth,
the same mouth he'd used to caress the most intimate
portions of Alex's body, locked to Eileen's. And then to
learn Mark and Shelby had a little something going on
the side as well. Mark Jordan was a perverted monster.
How could she have been so stupid, so blind?

The bedroom door opened silently on well-oiled
hinges. Dixon tensed, half expecting to see the felonious
Santa silhouetted in the doorway. When he realized who
it was, his heart beat faster, but not with fear. "Alexandra?" Was she sleepwalking?

She glided to the side of the bed, silent as a wraith,
her pale silk nightgown ghostly in the moonlight.
"Dixon?" Her voice was faint. "Did I wake you?"

"No. What's wrong? Did you hear something?"
Dixon rolled to his side, propping himself on an elbow.
The air was chill on his bare arms and chest.

"I can't sleep. I just keep remembering. . . ."

Dixon captured her fluttering hands and pulled her
down on the edge of the bed.

She slumped against him, burying her face against his
chest, her breath warm on his skin. "Hold me, Dixon.

Please hold me. I'm so confused. I don't know where to turn, whom to trust."

Moving over, he pulled her legs up onto the bed and wrapped the quilt around her. Alexandra's skin was cool to the touch. He wondered how long she'd been wandering around the apartment, fighting this battle on her own. Dixon enveloped her in warmth, chafing her chilly flesh and murmuring soothing phrases.

In the beginning, his intentions were completely honorable. Then, suddenly, things changed. One minute he was concentrating solely on comforting her. The next, he was all too aware of the silken length of her legs, the soft fullness of her breasts.

She shivered and clutched at his shoulders.

Muscles bunching, he shuddered and pulled her closer, pressing hot kisses to one satiny shoulder, then up the length of her neck.

Belatedly realizing where this was leading, he stopped.

"Oh, Dixon." Alexandra sighed and shifted, her mouth seeking his, her lips soft and yielding.

He responded cautiously, afraid to reveal the depth of his hunger for fear of scaring her off. *She's been hurt. She's just seeking comfort, not a relationship.*

She broke off the kiss with a breathy sigh, then snuggled closer, her hands splayed against his chest, her head tucked beneath his chin. "I'm so cold, Dixon, and you're so warm."

Warm? More like hot. Dixon took a deep breath, then exhaled slowly, battling to get his raging emotions under control. God, he ached for her. He'd never wanted a woman this much in his life.

So take what you want, urged his libido. *She wants it just as much as you do.*

She doesn't know what she wants. You represent safety to her in a world turned upside down. She's hurt and confused, argued his conscience.

She didn't feel confused. She felt good—no, perfect—rounded in all the right places. Their bodies fit together like puzzle pieces. Despite his good intentions, he found himself exploring the curves and hollows.

She moaned, her fingers clenched in his hair.

He froze, guiltily aware of his hand on her hip. Dammit, he was slime. He was pond scum, taking advantage of her this way. "I'm sorry, Alexandra. I didn't mean to—"

She turned onto her back, staring steadily up at him. "I want you, Dixon." She traced the line of his jaw with her fingertips. "I hurt so bad, like I'm bleeding inside. Can you understand that?"

He understood all right. Despite Brittany's betrayal, he'd damn near hemorrhaged to death when she left.

"I'm tired of the pain, tired of being scared all the time. I feel safe with you." Alexandra's smile was bittersweet.

Something twisted in his gut, something that had nothing to do with desire. God, he'd do anything . . . anything . . . to erase that expression from her face.

"I need you, Dixon. I need you and I want you." She slid one hand down over his tense stomach muscles, then lower, until she reached the elastic waistband of his shorts. Sliding her hand beneath, she found his erection.

"Please?" Her whisper shivered down his spine like an electric shock. Her touch was exquisite torture.

Groaning, he pulled her on top of him. One narrow

strap had slipped off her shoulder and he pushed it lower still, then peeled the silk away to reveal one full breast, its tip puckering in the cool air. Alexandra was so damned beautiful, the most beautiful woman he'd ever known.

Dixon closed his eyes, breathing in the intoxicating scent of her. Perfume? he wondered. Shampoo? Pheromones?

Her skin was warm silk beneath his hands. He felt dizzy, a victim of sensory overload. So soft, so sweet. Dixon nuzzled her breast, then drew her nipple into his mouth. He would never get enough of her, not in a thousand lifetimes.

She made an inarticulate sound deep in her throat, and he paused, his mouth at her breast. Had he hurt her? "What is it?"

Alexandra wriggled to a sitting position and pulled her nightgown over her head, tossing it behind her. "Nothing. Just getting comfortable." Her smile set the blood pounding thickly through his veins.

"Good idea." He added his shorts to the discard pile.

"Excellent," she agreed. She bent slowly nearer until her nipple nudged his lips in a silent invitation.

With a groan, Dixon gave himself up to the pleasure, immersing himself in sensation. Time and place ceased to exist. The universe narrowed to Alexandra, only Alexandra, and she was enough.

At first he thought the ringing in his ears was some weird by-product of passion. It was only when Alexandra's pliant body went rigid under his hands that he came out of the fog far enough to figure out what was really going on. *Oh, hell, not now.*

SEVEN

The telephone rang with annoying persistence. Alex, intoxicated by Dixon's kisses, drugged by his touch, forced her eyes open. "The phone," she said, pulling away from him. Someone had lousy timing. She squinted at the digital clock on the bedside table. Ten thirty-two.

"Ignore it." Dixon pressed his lips to her wrist.

Despite the shivers the kiss sent down her spine, she wriggled free. "Might be important. I'll be right back." She touched his mouth briefly with her own. "Promise."

Wrapping herself in an afghan, Alex slipped into the living room in time to pick up on the fourth ring. "Hello?"

No answer.

"Hello?"

For a moment she thought the line was dead. Then the harsh blare of a recording assaulted her ear. She recognized the song: "Santa Claus Is Coming to Town." The tape cut out as abruptly as it had started.

"Who is this?" she demanded.

She heard a click. Then the phone went dead.

Puzzled, she hung up.

The phone rang again almost immediately and she snatched at the receiver. "Who is this? What do you want?"

The caller ignored her frightened questions. "Which are you, Ms. Roundtree? Naughty or nice?"

The androgynous whisper set her heart beating wildly. Shivering, she hung up.

"What's wrong?"

Alex jumped at the sound of Dixon's voice. She swallowed hard, then turned to face him. "A crank caller."

He frowned, looking formidable despite the flowered sheet he was wrapped in. "What did he say?"

She shook her head. "Nothing that made sense." She described the calls.

"Did you recognize his voice?"

"No, it was muffled, but whoever it was knows me. This number's unlisted."

Dixon's frown deepened.

"Santa?" Her voice shook.

He nodded. "Who else?"

"But why?"

"To keep you off balance."

She made no response. What was there to say?

The phone shrilled and Alex stared at it in horror.

"Want me to get it?" Dixon stood with his hand poised above the receiver.

She closed her eyes for a second. "Please."

He answered on the second ring. "Yes? Yes. No, she's right here." He covered the mouthpiece with his palm. "For you," he whispered. "It's Jordan." He handed her the phone, his expression unreadable.

Not now. Reluctantly, she pressed the receiver to her ear. "I don't want to talk to you, Mark."

"Darling, what's wrong? Is your headache worse? Reggie told me about your accident and explained why you left the party early. You should have mentioned it when I stopped by to pick you up. But then, your *body-guard*"—he gave the word sarcastic emphasis—"wouldn't let me drive you to the party."

"Your T-bird is a two-seater and you refused to ride in his Jeep."

"Yano could have followed us. We haven't had five minutes alone together since you hired him."

"Dixon's only doing his job." Anger simmered just below the surface of Alex's words.

Mark cleared his throat. When he spoke again, all the sarcasm and irritation were gone. "Is something wrong, baby? Do you want me to come over?"

"No."

"Are you sure? You sound odd, almost angry."

"Not almost angry, Mark. Totally angry. I saw you in the library with Eileen."

"Yes?" He seemed puzzled. "She had to talk to me. Ed decided to postpone announcing the partnership, but according to Eileen, I've still got the inside track."

"When I walked into the library, you weren't talking."

"What were we . . . oh! So that's why you're upset. Look, Alex, that was nothing. Eileen caught me under the mistletoe and demanded a kiss. That's all there was to it. Cross my heart."

"What I saw was no peck on the cheek."

"Darling, you aren't jealous of Eileen, are you?" Mark gave a bark of incredulous laughter. "She's old enough to be my mother. You know me better than that."

"I thought I did." Her voice was clipped and cold.

"But darling—" he protested.

"I know what I saw, and that kiss wasn't as casual as you're pretending."

"Okay, listen, honey. Here's the way it is. Eileen's a player. Right now she has the hots for me. I admit it. And yes, I play along with her—to a point. She has a lot of influence with Ed. You know how important that promotion is."

"How far do you intend to go to win a partnership, Mark? All the way to the bedroom?"

"Don't be ridiculous."

"Ridiculous?"

"Oh, come on, Alex. Get off your high horse. Maybe Eileen and I push the boundaries a little, but I swear I'd never sleep with her. It's a flirtation, Alex. A harmless flirtation."

"Obviously we define *flirtation* somewhat differently."

"Dammit, I suppose you've never looked at another man. What about that so-called bodyguard of yours?"

Guilt washed over Alex. Not only had she looked, she'd touched. "What about him?"

"He's behind this, isn't he? What did he tell you?"

"Why? Got a guilty conscience?"

Mark was silent for a moment.

Alex clutched at the afghan trying to slide off her shoulders. She listened to Dixon rummaging through cupboards in the kitchen. Starving, no doubt. He'd missed dinner.

"Alex, I've seen the way Yano looks at you. He wants you, and I suspect he'd lie to get you."

"Lie?"

"About me. Tell you things to turn you against me. He may be working for you, honey, but he has his own agenda. He knows about your trust fund."

Alex felt cold. "Money? You think money motivates Dixon?"

"Don't be naive, Alex. Money motivates everyone."

She chewed at her lower lip. "You too?"

"Hey, I'd have fallen for you even if you were penniless, darling, but the cash is a nice bonus. I never pretended otherwise. It means we'll be able to start out on the right foot, buy a house in the Loomises' price range—hell, in the Loomises' neighborhood. Money is freedom, Alex. It's vacations on the Riviera and hired help. It's a Porsche in the garage and caviar whenever you want."

"I don't like caviar."

"That's not the point. The point is, I love you. Don't listen to anyone who tries to convince you otherwise."

"If you love me, then what were you doing with Shelby at Mother's party?"

Mark swore.

"And with Eileen tonight?"

"Honey, I already explained that. The kiss meant nothing to me. Eileen Loomis means nothing to me. You, on the other hand, mean everything."

"And Shelby?"

"What about her? You know we can't stand each other."

"Then what were the two of you doing locked inside my mother's bedroom?"

"I don't know what the hell Yano told you, but I swear I wasn't anywhere near Shelby."

"I'd like to believe you, Mark." She stared at her ring.

"Then believe me, darling. Look, we need to talk face-to-face. I'm coming over."

"No!" Her protest was instinctive.

"Why not?"

"It's late. I was just about to go to bed."

"Sounds like a great idea to me. I'll spend the night at your place, and you can give your bodyguard the night off."

"Mark, no. I'm confused. I need time to think."

He fell silent again. "All right," he said at length. "I understand. But I want you to think about this: I love you, Alex. I love you with all my heart. You're the woman I want to spend the rest of my life with. Think about that, will you?"

Was she wrong about Mark? His version of the truth was plausible, if not totally convincing. She sighed. "I'll think about it."

Dixon looked up as she entered the kitchen. "Sandwich?" He held a plate out to her. "Tuna salad. My specialty."

She shook her head and moved to the refrigerator. Pulling out the orange juice, she poured herself a glass.

"What did Jordan want?" It was none of his business, but he had to ask. She looked sick, even worse than she had after discovering her fiancé with another woman.

"He called to see how my headache was." She paused, staring down at the diamond on her left hand.

When she looked up, her expression was tortured. "Dixon, what happened tonight . . . what almost happened . . ." She dropped her gaze, flushing painfully. "I . . . there's no excuse for what I did. All I can say is I'm sorry and it won't happen again."

"Alexandra—" he started, but she cut him off.

"No, don't say anything. God, this is embarrassing! I'm so ashamed of myself." She bit her lip. "What I did tonight was unforgivable. I used you, Dixon."

"There was more to it than that," he said quietly. And if she thought any differently, she was lying to herself. He stared at her, willing her to look at him, but she kept her eyes carefully averted.

Alexandra sipped her juice. "Tomorrow, it might be better if you moved your stuff back downstairs to the break room."

"You're the boss." He took a bite of his sandwich, chewed, and swallowed. The tuna and bread might as well have been sawdust and cardboard. "What shall I do about the crank calls?"

"Report them to the police in the morning." She set her half-empty glass on the counter. "I'm going to bed."

Alone. She didn't say the word, but he heard it in the tone of her voice. So it was over before it began, and Dixon wasn't sure of anything except the fact that he was in desperate need of another cold shower.

Business finally slacked off about two. Alex cornered Mandy in the break room, where her twin was systematically picking all the blueberries from a muffin.

"If you don't like blueberries, why don't you eat the plain muffins?"

"I like the blueberry flavor," Mandy explained, licking her fingers one by one. "I just don't like the berries themselves."

"You're making a mess."

"So? I'll clean it up. I always do. What's eating you?"

"I need some advice."

Mandy perked up. "Oh, yeah? What about?"

"Dixon."

Mandy paused in mid-chew, staring at Alex wide-eyed. "Whaddabout'm?"

"Don't talk with your mouth full. It's disgusting."

Mandy swallowed. "What about him?" she repeated, more clearly this time.

"I kissed him last night."

"Way to go, Alex!" Mandy grinned from ear to ear.

Alex frowned. "I thought Mark was cheating on me."

"So seeking to assuage your wounded ego, you made a move on Dixon. Very sensible." After examining a portion of muffin for stray blueberries, Mandy stuffed it in her mouth.

Alex sighed. "Very stupid, you mean."

"What happened? Did he get all noble and spurn you?"

"No, he . . . well, never mind that. The thing is, I liked what I felt with Dixon. It was different. Special."

"So far, this doesn't sound like a problem, Alex. Dump Mark and go after Dixon. Where's the down-side?"

"Well, after Dixon and I had kissed and . . ."

"Whatever," Mandy supplied.

"We didn't go all the way," Alex said quickly.

"Bummer." Mandy nibbled at another section of muffin.

Alex could feel her cheeks flushing. "We probably would have, but the phone rang."

Mandy ran her eyebrows up and down. "Next time, unplug the stupid phone."

"I don't think there's going to be a next time."

"I'm confused. Why not? I thought you said you liked it."

"I did. It was wonderful. He was wonderful." Alex felt her color rise again.

Mandy's mouth fell open. "Oh, my God. This isn't just a sexual thing, is it? You're falling in love, aren't you?"

"Don't be absurd. How can I be in love with Dixon when I'm engaged to Mark?"

Mandy frowned. "I thought you said Mark cheated on you."

"No, I said I thought Mark had cheated on me, only I may have been wrong."

Mandy stirred the pile of rejected blueberries with one sticky finger. "Or maybe not. I've heard things. Mark's former mother-in-law is on the library board with me." She paused. "But Mark seemed so devoted to you, I dismissed her comments as gossip. After all, he'd have to be a moron to risk losing that trust fund."

Alex's stomach muscles clenched. "You think Mark's only after my money?"

Mandy stuffed another chunk of muffin in her mouth and chewed thoughtfully, studying her sister the whole time. "I didn't say the money was the only attraction. You have plenty of wonderful attributes, though it would sound like bragging if I enumerated them all." She grinned. "Hey, except for our weird eyes, we're a couple of babes."

"Mark says he loves my eyes."

"Tom says he loves my eyes too. Of course, it's more believable coming from a color-blind man." She popped the last bit of muffin in her mouth.

"You're not helping, Mandy. You know how self-conscious I am about them."

Mandy gave her a nasty look. "Oh, puh-leeze. You're talking about a slight genetic aberration. Emphasis on the slight. There's nothing wrong with your looks. You're not exactly a carnival sideshow, you know. In fact, your eyes lend a little character to that otherwise insipidly beautiful face."

"Quoting Tom again?"

Mandy licked her fingers. "Nah. Mother."

.

Drago felt his manhood stiffen as he watched the naked girl cavort under the waterfall. Though other native women were as lithe and lovely as this one, he'd never before seen a Tahitian with such fair hair. It hung in heavy golden waves, falling nearly to her waist. A stray lock fell forward to caress one voluptuous sun-kissed breast . . . just as he longed to do himself.

Why not indulge his longing? He hadn't had a woman in months, and this one stirred his fancy. She had the body of a temptress and the face of an angel. And all that hair, looking just as he'd fantasized Lady Arabella's would look en déshabille. Not that this girl was in any way the equal of the aristocratic Lady Spencer, despite her golden hair. No doubt the luxuriant blonde tresses were the legacy of some passing sailor. English or perhaps Scandinavian. The females in this part of the world were known to be remarkably free with their favors, regardless of the male's nationality.

*He stepped from the shadows and watched the girl's eyes
change as she took in the details of his appearance. Smiling, she
extended her arms in welcome. Remarkably free, he thought.
And he was remarkably needy. . . .*

Alex tossed the book across the room. *Drago's Woman*
landed faceup on the hearth, where Drago himself, bare-
chested and swashbuckling as all get-out, stared boldly
up at her from the cover.

"Bored?" Dixon, who was channel-surfing from the
sofa, the remote in one hand and a can of Coors in the
other, glanced at her, looking too damn much like Captain Drago for Alex's peace of mind.

She uncurled herself from the big armchair, stood,
and stretched. "Excruciatingly. What's on TV?"

He set the beer on the coffee table and consulted the
TV Guide. "News, news, and more news, infomercial on
a sensational breakthrough skin-care formula, the last
twenty minutes of *Holiday Inn,* pro wrestling, *Lifestyles,* or
America's Most Wanted. What's your pleasure?"

"None of the above." Alex chewed at her lower lip.
She hated to go to bed. It was only a little after ten and
she didn't feel the least bit sleepy.

"We could play games." Dixon's suggestion sounded
innocent enough, but his eyes sparkled with mischief.

"I don't think so."

"How 'bout I stick in a video?"

"Which one?"

His smile did weird things to her insides. "I noticed
earlier you have my favorite Christmas movie on tape."

She tried to think of what Christmas movies she had:
*Home Alone, The Santa Clause, How the Grinch Stole
Christmas,* and *Miracle on 34th Street.* Not a huge selec-
tion. She shrugged. "Whatever appeals to you."

As Dixon dug through the cabinet in the TV stand, a buzzer sounded. "What's that?" He stiffened.

"Someone's at the back door."

"I'll get it." He sprang to his feet in one sinuous movement, grabbing up the snub-nosed .38 from the coffee table. "Lock the door after me and don't open it unless you hear my voice."

"What? No password?" she teased.

Dixon raised an eyebrow. "I'm just trying to do my job."

She dropped her gaze. "I know. Joking is my way of coping with a terrifying situation." She spoke calmly, but her hands were balled into fists. "Anyway, it's probably just Mandy or my mother. I don't think the bad guys bother to ring the bell."

He grinned crookedly. "Yeah, no doubt you're right, but better safe than sorry." He passed her a tape, then hefted the revolver thoughtfully. "Why don't you start the movie?"

Alex glanced down at the tape. "*Die Hard*? *Die Hard* is your favorite Christmas movie?"

Dixon didn't hear her. He'd already disappeared down the stairs.

He reappeared moments later, a frown on his face. "I thought I told you to lock the door after me."

"I was going to—" She broke off as another man followed Dixon into the room. Officer Rios was out of uniform and for a minute Alex didn't recognize him.

"I was in the neighborhood," he said in answer to her questioning look. "Thought I'd see how you were doing."

Alex gave him a warm smile. "How kind of you."

"Yeah, real kind." Dixon spat the words out as if they tasted bad.

Cesar grinned at his friend. "Hey, man. What can I say? To serve and protect is my motto. Besides, my date terminated a little earlier than planned."

"Headache?" asked Dixon with a knowing smile.

Cesar shook his head. "Husband. Showed up unexpectedly."

"Big guy?"

Cesar grunted. "Long-haul trucker about six-four and three hundred pounds. Swear to God, I had no idea she was married. The lady forgot to mention it, and dumb me, I forgot to ask."

"Tough." Dixon didn't sound overly sympathetic.

"Have a seat." Alex waved toward the sofa. "We were just about to stick in a video."

Cesar tossed his jacket over a chair back, then made himself comfortable in the center of the sofa. He picked up the movie Alex had laid on the coffee table. "*Die Hard*. Yes! My favorite Christmas movie."

"What a coincidence. It's Dixon's favorite too."

Dixon shot her an imploring look.

She knew what he wanted. He wanted her to get rid of his friend. Too bad. She shoved the movie into the VCR, then sat down on one side of Cesar. She had no intention of discouraging Officer Rios. With him there, she felt much safer.

Not, she admitted to herself, that she doubted Dixon's ability to protect her from an outside threat. She had every confidence in his competence. What she doubted was her own ability to keep her hands to herself. With Cesar there, she wasn't likely to embarrass herself by doing anything silly—like throwing herself on Drago's—no, Dixon's—manly chest.

"By the way, Dix, we got the ballistics report on the slug we dug out of the back wall of your office."

"Yeah?"

"A .357 Magnum."

"What?" Alex stared. "You mean it was a handgun?"

"Probably. Why?"

She took a deep breath. "Because I own one. Half shares anyway. A stainless-steel Ruger Security Six, a present from Mother when Mandy and I opened the store. Protection in case anyone tried to rob us."

"Where do you keep it?" Suddenly Cesar was all business.

"The drawer under the cash register. Come on. I'll show you." They all trooped down to the office. The drawer was empty.

Cesar narrowed his eyes. "Who knew you kept a gun?"

"Who didn't? It was hardly a secret." Alex fought the panic that threatened to overwhelm her. *Her own gun.* Someone had tried to kill her with her own gun.

EIGHT

A shrill keening woke Dixon. He fumbled for the alarm button in the dark until it dawned on him that the sound wasn't coming from the clock. Three-forty. Too damn early for the alarm to go off. So what the hell was making that racket?

Smoke detector!

He sat up abruptly, disoriented until he remembered where he was—banished to the break room. With the door closed, the smoke wasn't too bad. He assumed it must be a lot heavier in the main showroom to have triggered the alarm.

He dressed in seconds, then stuffed his bare feet into running shoes, not bothering with socks, not stopping long enough to tie the laces.

Alexandra. He had to get Alexandra out of the apartment before it was too late.

The door wasn't hot to the touch. He kept his head well enough to remember to check before easing it open. No flames lit the darkness beyond, either, but the air was heavy with smoke. Choking back a cough, Dixon slammed the door shut. He wouldn't last long without something over his face. Moving quickly, he stripped the pillow and dropped the pillowcase in the stainless-steel sink in the corner. He turned the water on full blast, soaking the percale. Then, with the sopping cloth wrapped around his head, he ventured into the main showroom once again.

The back wall was ablaze. He couldn't see the fire through the thick black smoke, but he could hear its roar and feel its heat. Despite the danger, he moved closer. The door to the stairs was back there. If he couldn't get to the second floor, Alexandra didn't have a chance.

The doorknob burned his fingers, a tangible warning of what awaited him on the other side of the thick oak panels. His brain registered the futility of proceeding further, but his heart wasn't listening.

Using the pillowcase to protect his hand, he turned the knob. A mistake.

Heat exploded through the open door like a blow from the devil's fist, slamming him back twenty feet before laying him out on the floorboards. No use. Only a raging tunnel of smoke and flames remained. The stairs were gone. Just as he'd be gone, too, if he didn't get the hell out of there.

Choking, blinded by the smoke, he crawled toward what he hoped to God was the front door, keeping low, trying to suck enough precious oxygen into his burning lungs to keep his brain functional. If he lost consciousness now, before he escaped . . .

Dixon found the door with his head, slamming into the frame hard enough to rattle the glass. Dazed, he reached up instinctively to release the bolt. The mechanism gave with a ping and he crawled out into the cold.

He sprawled on his back in the slushy snow that lay two inches deep on the sidewalk, and fought to drag oxygen into his heaving lungs. Wet flakes landed on his face. He heard sirens in the distance. Alexandra must have called the fire department.

Alexandra. Oh, God! Alexandra! Rolling over, he shoved himself to his knees, then staggered to his feet.

He stared up at the two-story building. A reddish glow lit the rear, but the front was dark and deceptively peaceful looking. Inside Alexandra was trapped, perhaps already overcome by the deadly fumes. Where were the damn firefighters?

Scaling the old building's brick facade was a piece of cake, given the thickness of the decorative trim around the front windows. Pumped up on adrenaline, he probably could have run straight up the face of Yosemite's El Capitán.

Balancing on the narrow stone ledge, he pounded the glass with the heel of his hand, nearly losing his balance when the next window over blew out in a shower of glass.

A heavy oak chair crashed onto the sidewalk. Alexandra's head and shoulders, wreathed in smoke and framed by jagged shards of broken glass, appeared in the opening.

He sagged in relief and came within an ace of falling on top of the poor, battered chair. "You okay?" Which was a pretty stupid question to ask of a woman who sounded as if she were in the terminal stages of emphysema.

She shook her head. "No, but I will be." Using a fist wrapped with the folds of an afghan, she knocked out the remaining glass, then padded the windowsill with the coverlet.

"Here, grab my hand." Hanging on to a corner of the molding, he stretched an arm toward her.

"No, I have a ladder." She coughed in great gasping wheezes. "My mother's idea." More coughing. "If only I can get the damn thing hooked." Behind her, flames flared up with a whoosh. Her Christmas tree went up like a torch. "Oh, jeez."

Dixon inched along the ledge and levered himself inside. One end of the ladder was designed to loop over a couple of hooks fastened to the underside of the window frame, but the loops weren't quite big enough for the hooks. Dixon's heart measured the seconds as he fought the stubborn nylon. "Got it!" He locked the ladder in place and tossed the free end out the window. The bottom rung reached only two thirds of the way to the sidewalk.

Alexandra's face mirrored his own dismay. "Damn," he said softly. Then: "Don't worry. I'll go first."

Dixon dropped from the last rung, fighting to keep his balance on the slippery sidewalk. He went down on one knee but managed to regain his feet in time to catch Alexandra before her bare feet touched the slush.

She was wearing the same filmy pink nightgown she'd discarded so unceremoniously the night before, seemingly oblivious to the way it gaped at the neck and rode up on her thighs, baring an immodest amount of gooseflesh-covered skin to the chill night air. Still coughing and hacking from all the smoke she'd inhaled, she wrapped her arms around his neck and burrowed against his chest.

Backing them off to a safe distance from the burning

building, Dixon watched smoke pour from the broken window and open front door. Whipped by the draft, flames shot up from the roof and licked greedily at the contents of the showroom floor. Baskets, cuckoo clocks, music boxes, quilts—all were gobbled up by the voracious inferno. A muffled crash and a shower of sparks marked the collapse of a rafter in the rear of the building. Simultaneously, the Christmas window display burst into flame. Tinsel flared briefly before sizzling to blackened threads. The reindeer ignited in a domino effect, with Rudolph as the grand finale.

Alexandra mumbled something into his shirt.

"What?" He bent nearer, struggling to hear her over the screaming sirens of the approaching fire trucks.

When she turned toward him, the blank look on her face frightened him. "Santa really meant business this time," she said in an oddly uninflected voice.

"Alexandra?" A shiver rippled down his spine. "Alexandra?"

She stared wide-eyed, expressionless, as the devouring flames sent flickering shadows across her face.

Dixon shivered, more with apprehension than cold. "Are you all right, Alexandra?"

"All right?" A section of the roof collapsed with a roar. She laughed bitterly. "No, I'm not all right. Are you crazy? I just lost my home, my business, everything!"

"Not quite everything, sweetheart." Dixon brushed the hair back off her forehead. "You didn't lose your life."

"Not this time."

Dixon held her. For the moment it was all he could do.

"Where are you taking me?" Alex asked Dixon for the third time in ten minutes, hoping the repetition would wear him down. Though they'd spent what was left of the night at Regina's house, Alex had refused to jeopardize her mother's safety by staying any longer. Consequently, Dixon had arranged for them to hide out elsewhere. His stubborn refusal to tell her exactly where was driving her crazy.

Dixon didn't answer, though he did take one hand off the steering wheel long enough to lower his sunglasses and smirk at her over the top of the frames.

"You're the most irritating man I ever met."

"Oh, yeah? I thought your fiancé held that title. Did you ever get through to him?"

"No." Alex frowned. She'd called Mark's home number repeatedly from her mother's house, sure he'd be frantic with worry when he heard about the fire. But neither he nor his machine had answered.

"Do you need to stop anywhere before we leave Brunswick?"

She jumped on that. "We're leaving Brunswick?"

He gave a noncommittal grunt, swerving to avoid a teenager who darted out into the street from between two parked cars.

Startled, Alex turned toward the kid, a grungy-looking specimen in a baseball jacket and baggy pants. She scarcely noticed when he forked her the bird, though, her attention focused instead on the red Thunderbird in the parking lot of the Pioneer Inn. "Stop, Dixon!"

"Why?"

"Just pull in here next to the motel coffee shop."

"Hungry already?"

Not hardly. Her stomach rolled. The sports car in front of the end unit was Mark's. She'd bet her trust fund on it.

Dixon parked in an empty slot near the coffee-shop entrance. "What's going on, Alexandra?"

Before he had time to turn off the engine, she jumped out, making a beeline for the T-bird. She heard Dixon's footsteps pounding the pavement behind her.

"Alexandra, wait! Where are you going?"

Ignoring him, she gulped cold air in a vain attempt to quell the churning in her gut. She was practically across the lot before he caught up with her.

"Alexandra? What is it?" Dixon's voice seemed to echo in her ears. *What is it? What is it? What is it?*

"Mark's car." Her own voice sounded peculiar, harsh, ragged. She stared at Dixon's hand on her forearm, her only link to sanity in a strange, surrealistic world. If his watch had suddenly melted and dripped off his wrist into a puddle on the pavement, she wouldn't have been the least bit surprised.

Dixon tightened his grip. "Where?"

Alex jerked her head toward the car. "The bastard's shacked up with someone. That's why he didn't answer his phone." She looked up, half expecting him to tell her she was wrong, but the sadness in his gaze only reinforced her worst suspicions.

"You don't know which room he's in, and you can't very well go knocking on every door."

"No need." Tugging herself free, she ran toward the door from which Mark had just emerged.

He didn't see her at first. He was too busy flirting

with his companion, a blonde Alex didn't recognize. "Mark?"

He looked up at the sound of her voice. His face paled, then flushed bright red. "Alex! What are you doing here?"

"I'd ask you the same, but I already have a pretty good idea."

"Who's Mark?" The blonde looked up at him in confusion. "I thought you said your name was Jason."

"His name is mud!" Alex spat the words, then ripped the diamond from her finger and threw it at his face.

He ducked and the ring hit the brick wall behind him. "Alex, let me explain."

"What's to explain? You cheated on me. End of story. End of story and end of engagment."

"But darling—"

She sensed Dixon's presence behind her even before he spoke. "Don't you get it, Jordan? She's not your darling anymore. You screwed up."

"Up, down and sideways," said the blonde. "You low-down, scum-sucking piece of trash!" She thwacked him with her purse.

Alex would have enjoyed the shell-shocked look on Mark's face if she hadn't felt so wretched.

"Let's go." Dixon tugged gently at her arm.

"No, Alex. Please, you've got to listen to me! I can explain everything!"

"I'm not interested in your explanations," she told Mark. "I'm not interested, period." She turned and left without a backward glance.

"Why, Dixon? Why'd he do it?" They'd been driving almost half an hour. She gripped the dash tightly. The pale line at the base of her ring finger served as a mocking reminder of how close she'd come to making the biggest mistake of her life.

He shrugged. "Because he's a damn fool."

I'm no genius myself. "I believed him. The evidence was right there in front of me, but I believed him."

"Don't be too hard on yourself." Dixon reached over, laying his hand on top of hers. "Jordan's a good liar. He's had years of practice."

"I'm better off without him," she said. Just words. She didn't feel better. She didn't even feel good. They turned onto an unmarked road. "Where are we? This road doesn't look familiar."

"It's private."

"Across private property?"

He nodded.

"Your grandfather's private property," she guessed.

His lips quirked up in amused approval. "I'll make a detective out of you yet."

They turned down yet another ice-covered, unmarked gravel road. Alexandra studied the snowy landscape, rolling hills as far as the eye could see, the land fenced, but obviously not farmed. No sprinkler pipes or corrugates, just mile after mile of snow-covered sagebrush and bunchgrass. "How much farther?"

The look he gave her was almost pitying. "You don't expect me to answer that, do you?"

"Well, if we're not close, I'd appreciate it if you'd stop at the nearest sagebrush. I have to go."

He mumbled something under his breath.

"What?"

"We're almost there."

"Glad to hear it." Her smile was smug. "I guess the need to go gives me a legitimate 'need to know.'"

"I guess it does," he said dryly.

She chuckled. "Gotcha! I was exaggerating my urgency."

Dixon grinned. "Good, because I was exaggerating about almost being there."

Naturally, as soon as he said that, she realized she really did have to go. Damn him. Why was he being so secretive anyway?

"What's your middle name?"

He looked at her askance. "Why?"

"Why not? Don't tell me that's privileged information."

"No, but—"

"What's your middle name, then?"

He cleared his throat. "Actually, I have two middle names."

She twirled a hand as if she were trying to reel the information out of him. "And they are . . ."

Was he blushing? He was.

"Olaf, after one of my mother's favorite uncles." He paused.

"And?"

"And Kenichi after someone on my dad's side."

"So your full name is Dixon Olaf Kenichi Yano, right?"

"Right, though I can't see what my middle names have to do with anything."

"I am about to chew you out. And you can't chew someone out properly unless you use their full name. So hold on to your hat, Mr. Dixon Olaf Kenichi Yano." She took a deep breath. "I hired you to keep me safe, but—"

"And that's exactly what I'm trying to do."

"Don't interrupt! It throws off my rhythm. Okay, as I was saying, I hired you to keep me safe, but there's no reason to be so damn closemouthed. What do you think? I'm going to take out an ad in the paper announcing our whereabouts? I'm not completely stupid, you know. And I do have rights. This idiotic 007 routine of yours is driving me insane. You . . . you . . ." Alex stammered to a halt, unable to think of a fitting description.

"Arrogant jerk?" Dixon suggested helpfully.

"Yes!"

"Obnoxious snothead?"

"That too."

"Devious, secretive SOB?"

"Absolutely."

"Did I forget anything?"

"How about self-important small-town PI with an anachronistic J. Edgar Hoover complex?"

He winced. "Now, that hurts." He made quite a business of pulling an imaginary dagger from his heart.

His silliness forced a reluctant chuckle from Alex. "You're a hard man to stay angry with." She sighed. "But don't you think you're carrying secrecy too far? It's my life. Don't I have a right to know where we're going?"

"Okay. Since you put it that way. We're headed for my great-grandmother's house."

"Your great-grandmother lives out here in the boonies?"

"Right again. Place'll make an ideal hideout." The Jeep veered sideways. Dixon turned into the skid, correcting effortlessly. Alex knew she would have done a one-eighty and landed in a clump of sagebrush if she'd tried the same maneuver.

"How old is she?"

"A hundred three on her last birthday."

Alex took a second or two to digest the information. "A hundred three and living all alone out here? She must be healthy."

"Oh, yeah. All the Yanos are healthy as horses. Probably thanks to all the rice we eat. Don't worry. Great-grandmother's a kick."

Alex smiled nervously as the road dead-ended in front of a neat one-story ranch house with board and batten siding and a shake-shingle roof. The yard was immaculate, edged with topiaried shrubbery, several of which appeared to be cringing away from the tiny figure who tottered out the front door.

The ancient gnome of a woman, dressed in leggings and an oversized sweatshirt, approached Dixon's Jeep, gabbling rapidly in a high, shrill voice. Dixon got out, enveloping the old lady in a bear hug that swept her off her feet.

"How are you, Great-grandmother?"

His greeting loosed another spate of staccato syllables.

"This is my client Alexandra Roundtree."

The old lady's head bobbed energetically as she made her way around the car to grip Alex's hand between her tiny wizened paws.

Evidently she understood English, which was a relief since Alex really did need a bathroom now, and she was darned if she could think of a graceful way to mime that particular desire.

"Say hello," urged Dixon.

"*Ohayo.*" Proudly, Alex produced one of the gems of her very limited Japanese vocabulary.

"A lovely state," Dixon said with a grin.

Alex shot him a dirty look. Couldn't he see she was trying?

Soon, however, she regretted her polite attempt to greet her hostess in Japanese, as the old lady continued to pump away at Alex's hand while rattling off a string of incomprehensible syllables.

Alex shot Dixon a pleading look.

He shrugged.

"I'm sorry," she said when the old lady paused expectantly. "I don't understand Japanese."

Great-grandmother Yano dropped Alex's hand like a hot potato, turned, and shuffled off toward the house in a huff.

Alex held her hands out, palms up, fingers spread beseechingly. "What did I say?"

"You insulted her," he said. "She was speaking English."

Alex woke up with a start. The *Jeopardy* theme was playing in the background. Dixon was humming along. When she felt the vibrations buzzing in her ear, Alex realized the "pillow" beneath her head was really Dixon's chest. She sat up abruptly, scanning the tiny living room for Great-grandmother. What must the old woman think of her?

Evidently, not much. Great-grandmother was nowhere to be seen. Besides the sofa where she and Dixon sat, the only other seat, a wooden swing rocker, was occupied by what was either the world's ugliest fur coat or a pile of calico cats. Alex put her vote in for cats since she could count at least ten legs in various improbable positions.

"Quick," said Dixon. "The category is world geography. The highest and lowest altitudes in South America are both located in this country known for its salubrious air."

"I don't know. Peru? Bolivia? Somewhere in the Andes? Where's your great-grandmother?"

"Gone." He sounded distracted. "Salubrious air. Good air."

"Gone? Gone how? Gone where?"

He slapped his thigh. "Buenos Aires. Argentina!"

"Argentina?" Alex didn't think she'd heard him right.

Dixon tore his gaze from the TV. "I mean, 'What is Argentina?' That's the answer—or rather the question."

"What is Argentina?" echoed Alex Trebek. "That's absolutely correct. How much did you wager?"

"Not enough," scoffed Dixon. "The guy's a weenie. Now me, I'd have bet my wad and won too."

"Yeah, you're a regular whiz kid all right. Where's your great-grandmother?"

"I told you. Gone."

"Gone where?"

"California," Dixon answered.

"For how long?"

"All winter. I thought I explained that already."

"You didn't tell me anything."

"I didn't mention Great-grandmother Yano's yearly pilgrimage to visit her brother in Palo Alto? Great-great-uncle Taro's the baby of the family, a mere ninety-eight."

"You never said a word."

"Well, you should have figured it out. What did you think we were doing here?"

"Hiding from a would-be murderer-slash-arsonist?"

"That, too, of course, but also house-sitting."

Alex relaxed. "She really is gone, then? What a relief. After starting out on the wrong foot, I was worried I was going to have to eat raw fish just to redeem myself."

"Not this time of year," Dixon assured her. He gestured toward the television. "Jeez! What did I tell you? A measly hundred dollars. That wimp deserves to lose."

Alex yawned and stretched. "How long was I asleep anyway?"

"Almost five hours. You missed lunch. Hungry?"

"Starving."

"Great-grandmother's pantry's well stocked. How about I whip up my specialty, carp-head stew?"

"Sure. If you want." His specialty was carp-head stew? Alex bit her lip. "Sounds great." She stood up and padded sock-footed across the room to examine the cat pile. A raspy, asthmatic purr rewarded her tentative stroke of one splotchy head.

"That's Wynonna. Great-grandmother's a big fan of country music. All her cats are named for female vocalists."

Alex jumped at the sound of Dixon's voice. She hadn't realized he'd followed her. She turned and found herself staring at the buttons on his denim shirt.

Slowly she raised her eyes to meet his steady gaze. They stared at one another in silence for an endless moment. Alex wasn't sure what he saw in her face, but what she read in his reassured her. This was a man to trust, a man to depend on. *A man to love*, whispered her heart. If only . . .

She broke off eye contact, her gaze caught by the pale reminder at the base of her ring finger. If only she could trust her own judgment when it came to men. Mark had seemed the perfect man too. At first.

"You're thinking about Jordan, aren't you?"

Alex glanced at Dixon, surprised by the harshness of his tone. His mouth was tight with suppressed anger, but his eyes held only sadness. "Dixon—" she started, but he cut her off.

"None of my business."

Which meant what? That she'd only hired him as a bodyguard, not a shrink? That he didn't want to get involved in her personal problems? She studied Dixon's face, trying to interpret his expression.

"I didn't mean to upset you, Alexandra." He glanced up from the stove, where he was stirring a pot of something that smelled delicious. Her mouth watered.

She smiled faintly. "You didn't. Don't worry. I'm tougher than I look. I'll live." She moved closer to peer into the heavy stainless-steel soup pot. She had to admit fish-head stew smelled a lot more appetizing than it sounded. Maybe if she ate with her eyes closed, she could pretend it was beef stew. It sure smelled like beef stew. Dinty Moore beef stew, to be exact. "Where's the trash?" she demanded, suddenly suspicious.

"Under the sink. Why?"

Alex didn't answer right away. After rummaging briefly through the refuse, she held a can aloft in triumph. "Aha!"

"What?" Dixon raised an eyebrow, his expression mildly curious.

"It *is* Dinty Moore beef stew."

"So?" He shrugged. "I never claimed to be Julia Child." Slowly a smile lit his face. "Oh, I get it. You expected fish eyeballs staring back up at you."

"Well, you said—"

"I was joking."

"Oh."

"Why don't you set the table? The bowls are in the cupboard next to the sink and the silverware's in the top drawer at the end of the counter."

Alex did as he suggested.

"I think I may finally have a lead on who's after you." Dixon plopped a heavy crocheted pot holder in the center of the kitchen table and set the stew pot on it. "I wonder where Great-grandmother keeps her ladles."

Alex spied a ladle hanging from a wrought-iron rack above the center island. She handed it to Dixon. "Who's after me?"

"I'm not positive, but the evidence is fairly strong."

"Who?" she demanded.

"Danny Hall."

"You're kidding. That business happened so long ago. I really thought he was a long shot."

"Not so long. He's out of prison, has been for over a year. And guess what he does for a living?"

"He used to be in construction."

"Still is. Want to guess where he's working?"

She stared at him blankly. "The Stockton renovation?"

"Right. Directly across the street from my office."

"So maybe the reason the police didn't catch the shooter was because he never left the building."

"Bingo."

NINE

Dixon poured stew into Alexandra's bowl. Even with a worried frown wrinkling her forehead, she looked adorable.

"How did you find out about Danny Hall?" She poured herself a glass of milk.

Dixon passed her the bowl and began ladling stew for himself. "Cesar, of course. I gave him a list of suspects and he's been poking around, using his official contacts."

"What else did he find out? Beyond the fact that Hall's back working construction? Any arrests recently? Parole violations?"

Dixon sat down across from Alexandra. "Uh-uh. *Nada*. The guy hasn't had so much as a parking ticket since his release."

Alexandra blew on a spoonful of stew. "No rumors of domestic violence?" She took a cautious bite.

"No reports of any problems, though apparently he *is* living with someone. I wrote it down somewhere." He dug a crumpled scrap of paper from his hip pocket. "Wendy Calzacorta," he read. "Ever heard of her?"

Alexandra frowned. "I went to school with Tyler Calzacorta. He had a younger sister, too, but I think her name was Kim. I don't remember a Wendy. If she's mixed up with Danny Hall, though, she has my sympathy. He treated Julie like his personal punching bag." She shuddered. "The man's an animal." She laid her spoon aside and clasped her shaking hands together.

Dixon covered them with his own. Her trembling sparked a fierce protectiveness in him. "I won't let Hall hurt you."

Her gaze met his. "I know." A wobbly smile curved her lips, lips he longed to kiss.

I love you, Alexandra. He couldn't say the words. He didn't have the right. But he could think them. He could live them. He could and would keep her safe. No matter what.

Alex stared at the ceiling in Great-grandmother Yano's spare bedroom and listened to the wind. Beyond the confines of the snug little house, a blizzard raged, the wind howling like a pack of hungry wolves, ice crystals clawing and scraping at the windows.

For once, she didn't mind the snow. In fact, she welcomed it. Let it snow all night. Let it snow until the drifts piled up to the eaves, isolating her—them—from the outside world. From the danger. From whoever wanted her dead.

Danny Hall. She'd never liked him, never trusted him, not from the first time they'd met. Later, after she'd seen the way he treated Julie, that initial dislike had grown into an active loathing. And while it was true that Alex's testimony, along with that of a dozen other witnesses, had put Hall behind bars, she couldn't help wondering if that was sufficient motivation for murder. Would Danny Hall really have held a grudge for so long? Was he so vengeful, so full of rage that he wished her dead? Alex didn't want to believe it. How could he hate her enough to want to kill her? How could anyone?

Her heartbeat quickened. Her breathing grew rapid and shallow. Cold sweat beaded her forehead and upper lip. Panicked, she flicked on the bedside light and groped for her watch with shaking hands. A little after two and so far she hadn't had a wink of sleep.

Her mind raced, flitting from one memory to another, reliving the increasingly frightening events of the past few weeks: the accidents that weren't really accidents, the break-in, the shove that had sent her sprawling into the street in front of a car, the terrifying realization that she was trapped in a burning building.

The official verdict wasn't in yet, but she was convinced the fire had been arson. An ugly word, arson.

Her intestines tied themselves in knots. Not only arson, she realized, but attempted murder. Someone—Danny Hall?—wanted her dead. And with the exception of her mother and her paid bodyguard, no one seemed to care. Certainly not Mark.

Had he ever truly cared for her? Or had he been interested only in her money? *How could I have been so blind?*

Reaching up, she turned off the light, feeling less exposed, less vulnerable in the darkness.

Both Mandy and her mother had had their doubts

about Mark right from the start, but she'd refused to listen. Even Dixon had tried to tell her the truth. . . .

Dixon. His concern for her well-being went beyond any professional requirements. He cared for her. She could see it in his face, feel it in his touch.

His touch. Embarrassed by, and ashamed of, her own wanton behavior, Alex had tried not to dwell on the physical aspect of their relationship. But now, alone with her thoughts in the sheltering darkness, she examined her feelings. The truth was Dixon affected her in a way no man ever had. Was that love or lust? A wish for true commitment or raging hormones? She didn't know, and she was half-afraid to find out for fear of what that knowledge might do to her tidy little world.

Could she trust her own judgment? What if she was wrong about Dixon? She'd been so wrong about Mark.

Dixon awoke to the smell of frying bacon. He couldn't remember the last time he'd had bacon for breakfast. Cereal, milk, and a glass of juice was his usual bachelor fare. And on the rare occasions when he ate out, an Egg McMuffin was par for the course. The tantalizing odor of frying meat brought a reminiscent smile to his face. When he was a kid his mother had prepared special breakfasts on the weekends, sausage and waffles or bacon and eggs.

However, when he emerged from the bathroom fifteen minutes later, dressed in fresh clothes, his hair still damp from the shower, he found the house clouded with bluish smoke and a skillet full of blackened strips cooling on a back burner. Alexandra stood by the counter, her slender fingers pleating and unpleating the loose tail of the flannel shirt she wore over a white turtleneck. Her expression chilled his blood.

"What's wrong?" He touched her hand. It was cold and unresponsive. "Alexandra, what is it? What's happened?"

She swung around to face him, but her beautiful mix-and-match eyes were unfocused. "I burned the bacon."

His grip on her hand tightened. "Damn the bacon. That's not what upset you. Tell me, Alexandra. What else happened while I was in the shower?"

She looked at him then, really looked at him.

Dixon felt the impact of the connection like a physical blow. Emotion linked them. Her distress became his own. His muscles tensed against the onslaught. A mixture of pain and anger churned his gut. He tasted bile.

She took a little hitching breath. Her lips parted, but no sound emerged. She shook her head and cleared her throat. "I just did something very stupid."

She looked so miserable, Dixon pulled her into his arms, tucking her head under his chin.

"Don't worry. There's no law against stupidity."

She stood rigid in his arms, clutching him so tightly that her fingernails seemed to be cutting trenches in his back. "Maybe there should be." Releasing him, Alexandra sank down on the bar stool behind her. She stared at her clenched fists. "Mark—"

His name hung between them like a dark cloud.

Dixon lifted her chin. "What about Mark? You want me to put out a contract on him?"

Her startled gaze met his.

"A joke, Alexandra." He tapped the tip of her nose, then frowned. "Wait. You didn't do something really dumb like decide to forgive and forget?"

"No." Sighing sharply, she dropped her gaze to the countertop, where she traced the pattern in the Formica with one fingertip.

"Then what?" He outlined the curve of her lower lip.

"Mark. I called him just now."

"You what?"

"Go ahead. Yell at me, Dixon. Tell me what a fool I am."

A pool of silence enveloped them.

"What did he say?" he asked at last. "And more importantly, what did you say?" Damn it to hell and back, if she'd let that sweet-talking snake slither his way back into her good graces . . .

"All he said was"—Alexandra uttered a short bark of unamused laughter, never lifting her gaze from the countertop—" 'I can't come to the phone right now. Leave a message at the tone.' " She sounded as if she were strangling on the words.

"And you left a message?" he asked quickly.

She frowned. "Oh, yeah. I left a message all right. He has it all on tape."

Dixon stood silent at her side, waiting for her to go on.

Her smile was sheepish. "I called Mark Jordan every name in the book. And some not in the book."

The phone rang and they both jumped. Alexandra's eyes looked huge. "Who?"

"You didn't happen to mention where you were in the course of your tirade, did you?"

"No, but . . . oh, damn! I didn't think. Mark has caller ID." Alexandra braced her stockinged feet on the rung of the stool and stared at the ringing phone as if it were a rattlesnake ready to strike.

"Want me to take care of him for you?"

She shook her head. "He's my problem."

She closed her eyes for a second, then lifted the receiver.

"No, Mark. It's over," she said after a while. "I don't want to talk about it. And I don't want to listen to you talk about it. Not now. Not ever."

Dixon could hear the unintelligible gabble on the other end continuing unabated.

Shrugging, Alexandra gently returned the receiver to the cradle. "He never did listen to anything I said. Dixon, how could I have fallen for a man like that in the first place?"

He ran his fingertips across her furrowed brow. "Jordan puts up a good front."

She bit her lip. "And I'm a gullible idiot."

"No, Alexandra. He's the idiot." Dixon gathered her close.

She sighed, a hopeless sound.

He held her away from him. "Don't blame yourself for Jordan's infidelity. His actions had nothing to do with you and everything to do with feeding that voracious ego of his. Your only problem seems to be your talent for picking losers."

She gave a funny little hiccuping sob of laughter. "But how can I tell the losers from the winners? Men should come with warning labels, like cigarettes."

He laughed. "Women too."

"Are you speaking from experience?"

He clenched his jaw at the thought of Brittany. "Painful experience."

"Something you want to talk about?"

"Nothing to say. She claimed she loved me, but she

didn't. Once the money ran out, once she'd maxed out all my credit cards, once she'd bilked my grandfather out of fifty thousand dollars, she moved on."

"I'm sorry."

"I'm not. She taught me a lesson, one I'm not likely to forget in a hurry."

Alexandra studied his face, her expression tender.

Little by little the tension left Dixon, only to be replaced by a heightened awareness of the woman in his arms. To hell with Brittany. She was the past. Alexandra was the present.

"The truth is Mark hurt my pride more than my heart. I thought I loved him, but lately, even before I had reason to distrust him, I've been having a few doubts of my own." She stared at the buttons on his shirt. "Ever since I met you . . ."

Dixon's chest felt tight. What was she saying?

"But my judgment hasn't proved very reliable in the past." He could feel her trembling. "Like you said, I have a talent for picking losers." She bit down hard on her lower lip. "Does that mean if I picked you, Dixon, you'd turn out to be a loser too?"

His heart gave a lurch, but his answer came without hesitation. "Never." He caught her chin, tipped her face up to his, and kissed her long and deep. "Never," he whispered against her lips.

She pulled away, and he thought he'd blown it until he saw her face.

Her lower lip quivered, but her eyes shone. "In that case, I choose you, Dixon Olaf Kenichi Yano."

Dixon froze. Did she mean what he thought she meant? "Are you sure? Are you absolutely sure?"

"Yes. No. I don't know." Uncertainty rippled across her face.

Dixon put her gently away from him. "When you make up your mind, we'll talk. Until then . . ." He shrugged.

She looked startled. "I was trying to be honest. I'm a little confused."

"About me? You think I'm like Jordan?"

"No. I don't know." She swallowed hard. "Dixon, what's wrong? I thought . . ."

"What?"

She shook her head, making an inarticulate sound. "That there was something between us. That you had more than a professional interest in me. The way you look at me . . . the way you kissed me just now . . ." Her cheeks were pink.

He knew what this confession must be costing her, but he also knew it was essential to get things straight from the very beginning. Brittany had taught him that much. The hard way. Never again, he'd promised himself. Never again would he walk blindly into a relationship, especially not when he cared this much about the woman. Caring made a man vulnerable. And vulnerable was only another word for stupid.

"Up to now I've let you call all the shots." He spoke firmly, his voice coolly unemotional.

Alexandra studied him in silence, her lower lip caught between her teeth. She looked so damn sweet and sexy that he was tempted to take her right there on the kitchen floor and to hell with the ground rules.

Her smile brought his blood to a simmer. "Your point being?"

And so damn sassy, he added to his mental inventory. "It's my turn."

"Okay," she said slowly. "What does that mean exactly?"

"I want you."

"Likewise, I'm sure."

"I want you, but I'm not going to make any promises. Do you understand?"

"No promises?"

"Not a one. No diamond rings. No three-bedroom house with a thirty-year mortgage. No kids. No strings."

Alexandra smiled crookedly. "You know, Dixon, you really need to work on your line."

"It's not a line. I call it the ground rules."

"And I call it bull." Her eyes snapped. "You said Mark was an idiot? You're the idiot."

Tell me something I don't know. "Those are my terms. Take 'em or leave 'em."

Dixon watched various emotions flit across her expressive face. She might condemn him as an idiot, but she hadn't given up on him. Not yet.

Slowly a rueful smile tilted the corners of her mouth. "I didn't have much luck with my engagement. All the promises ended up being broken." Gnawing at her lip, she focused on her bare ring finger. Finally, after what felt like an eternity to Dixon, Alexandra seemed to make up her mind. She took a deep breath and turned to him. "So by your ground rules, what would you call this no-strings verbal contract you're proposing, Dixon? A nonengagement? A disengagement? An unengagement?" She nodded thoughtfully. "Yes, an unengagement. I like the sound of that." She smiled again, mischief in her eyes. "I, Alexandra, take you, Dixon, to be my unlawfully unwedded unhusband." She slid her arms around his neck.

Dixon grabbed her forearms. "Which brings us to my second condition."

Pressing her body to his, Alexandra nipped at his lower lip. "Have your lawyer talk to my lawyer, Yano."

"But you don't understand—"

She dragged his face down to meet hers and kissed him until his head swam.

"The ground rules," he protested, albeit feebly.

"Forget the ground rules. There's only one rule in an unengagement: There are no rules. Okay?"

"But—" He opened his mouth to argue the point and Alexandra immediately took advantage. Her soft lips and clever, darting tongue proved devastating to his train of thought.

"Oh, hell," he said with a groan.

When they broke apart, both of them gasping for air, Dixon lifted her into his arms and carried her to the living room. He settled on the sofa with Alexandra on his lap.

"Just like a romance hero." She traced his cheekbones with her fingertips.

"Oh, yeah? You think?"

"Definitely." She twisted around to sit astride him.

New sensations rocked his body, destroying what was left of his equilibrium. He throbbed with need.

"You're the sexiest man I ever met, Dixon"—she pushed him back against the cushions, pressing a soft kiss to his cheek—"Olaf"—another kiss, this one on his chin—"Kenichi"—she cradled his head between her hands; the tip of her tongue flicked across his upper lip—"Yano."

Her kiss began as a benediction, warm and gentle; it ended as a torment, hot and arousing.

Dixon groaned and pulled her closer. Tangling his fingers in her hair, he kissed her long and deep, unleashing the passion he'd controlled for so long. He needed Alexandra; he ached with the longing. But even with his brain fogged by desire, Dixon recognized that despite all his bravado about ground rules and conditions, this woman, this relationship, was different. *I love you, sweetheart.*

I love you, Dixon. The thought reverberated so loudly in her head, Alex was surprised Dixon couldn't hear it. She would have said the words aloud, but her mouth was otherwise engaged. No, make that married.

She wasn't entirely inexperienced, but Dixon's kiss—correction, his assault on her senses—had her on the verge of swooning like some Victorian virgin. Her skin was on fire, every nerve ending acutely sensitive to his touch.

Finally, starved for air, she broke off the kiss, leaning her forehead against Dixon's, drawing one ragged breath after another. He pressed quick, hot kisses to her cheeks and forehead, her chin and the tip of her nose, then slid his hands up to cup her breasts.

Startled, she opened her eyes to find him looking at her, his gaze intent and loving, yet somehow tinged with sadness. A wave of love and compassion welled up inside her. She trembled with the need to erase every vestige of unhappiness shadowing his heart. "Dixon?"

"It's all right, sweetheart." A faint smile curved his lips. Again he pressed his mouth to hers, kissing her with controlled deliberation as his thumbs stroked languorously back and forth across her nipples. Alexandra shut her eyes, concentrating on the pleasure.

Heat flooded her. She arched into his hands as he slid his tongue along the scalloped top edge of her bra. Where had the rest of her clothes gone? Although she didn't remember taking them off, her shirt and turtleneck had disappeared. Perhaps, she thought woozily, they'd evaporated in the heat.

Dixon flicked the front closure of her bra and pushed the lacy cups aside. She wriggled out of the straps.

"Look at me, Alexandra."

She opened her eyes to find him staring at her, his expression intent, his eyes soft, his mouth curved in a tender smile. "You're beautiful."

Music to her ears, strange, haunting music that wrapped itself around her heart. She shivered at the look on his face.

You're beautiful too. She touched the rugged line of his jaw, the angle of his cheekbones, the curve of his lips.

Dixon drew the tip of her finger into his mouth, sucking and nibbling.

She shivered again, feverish with excitement.

Dixon released her finger and slipped out of his sweatshirt. His body was as gorgeous as his face, lean and hard-muscled.

She splayed her hands against his chest, closing her eyes while she savored the textures of skin and hair, muscle and sinew. Fresh from the shower, he smelled of soap. She'd never suspected until now that Ivory could be such a turn-on. Oh, God, but she wanted him . . . needed him.

Dixon's breathing quickened. She felt the rapid rise and fall of his rib cage against her palms.

Suddenly he seized her wrists and pulled her arms around his neck, ducking his head to taste her breasts.

Alex moaned, arching closer. His mouth and tongue sparked pleasurable sensations, sensations echoed in her abdomen.

The friction of their remaining clothing only heightened her need. Damp and fully aroused, Alex craved release. If she didn't have him soon, she would disintegrate. "Dixon, please. I need you."

"Hold that thought." His breath was hot against her naked skin. Deftly he rolled her onto her back, stood up, kicked off his boots, and peeled off his jeans. His socks went flying and then his shorts.

Alex stared, tongue-tied, her thoughts incoherent.

His smile melted her bones. "Stand up," he said, "and I'll help you out of your clothes."

She drew a ragged breath. Giant economy size. Definitely giant economy size.

Dixon extended a hand, but she just shook her head. "I can't get up. My legs are noodly."

"No problem." He knelt beside her. "Want to see me undo the button with my teeth?"

"You can do that, huh?" If Alex had had a fan handy, she'd have used it. All of a sudden the oxygen supply in the room was totally inadequate for her needs.

"Oh, I'm multitalented." He proved his claim by stripping off her jeans and socks in two seconds flat. "Red toenails," he observed. "How seasonal." As his gaze slid slowly up her calves to her thighs and then her hips, his grin took on a distinctly devilish slant. "And red underwear, too, I see. Red silk French-cut bikini underwear."

"My mother bought them." She knew she sounded defensive.

He lowered his eyelids to half-mast. "Your mother has good taste. They're sexy as hell. You're sexy as hell." His voice rasped along her tingling nerves.

Lowering his head, Dixon pressed hot openmouthed kisses down her stomach.

Shuddering in delight, Alex buried her fingers in his hair.

He paused just long enough to flick her navel with his tongue before continuing his downward trek. When he reached the barrier of red silk, he lifted her hips, molding and squeezing the muscles of her buttocks before hooking his thumbs under the elastic of the waistband and stripping away the last barrier between them.

TEN

Dixon watched Alexandra's face change as his tongue invaded her warmth. Her eyes glazed over. She gasped and muttered something that might have been his name. It was hard to hear over the blood pounding at his temples.

Then she thrust upward, matching each deliberate foray of his tongue over and over until her body convulsed at last in shudders of ecstasy. "Oh, God. Dixon!"

He smiled in satisfaction, exulting in Alexandra's responsiveness, evidence of his power to please her. Her obvious delight made his own pleasure all the richer. *So beautiful. So precious.* He would keep her safe. No matter what.

"Dixon?" She was still breathing hard.

"I'm right here, sweetheart." He laid the back of his hand in the hollow between her breasts and felt her heart beating a mad tattoo against her breastbone.

Her eyes flew open at his touch. "That was . . . incredible." The look on her face made his own heart skip a beat. If ever a woman deserved to be loved . . .

"Enjoy yourself, did you?"

"Enjoyed *you*. I feel so . . . good. Good, but guilty." Her smile was tinged with sheepishness. "I had all the fun."

"Fun's not over yet." Dixon settled himself against the cushions at the other end of the sofa and dragged her unresisting form on top of him.

He delighted as much in the startled expression on her lovely flushed face as in the feel of her soft breasts pressing against his chest.

Gripping her hips, he lifted her into position. "Oh," she said in surprise as he slid inside. She fit him like a glove.

Alexandra sat up, adjusting herself to him, her wriggling movements pulling him deeper.

"Ah!" He gritted his teeth, battling for control. Gradually, he felt the tension ease.

Slowly he withdrew, then plunged back into her.

She arched her back in a reflexive gesture. Her nails bit into his shoulders. Surprise was written across her face. "I don't believe this," she whispered. "Not again. Not so soon."

She sat up, clenching her muscles around him.

Dixon groaned. He wouldn't last much longer at this rate. Everything about this woman was soft, her eyes, her lips, her breasts. He let his fingertips trail across her body, concentrating on the texture of her skin. Alexandra. Like hot silk under his hands.

When he touched her breasts, she shivered and her nipples responded instantly, the hard pink nubs swollen and erect against his fingertips.

"Oh, yes. There, Dixon. Touch me there."

Using his thumbs, he brushed back and forth across the sensitized skin while thrusting with his hips. He drowned his senses in the feel of her, the female fragrance of her. Alexandra. Her warmth filled all the cold, secret places, all the hidden, lonely places in his heart and mind and soul. Alexandra.

Suddenly she was moaning his name, sobbing for release.

His last shred of control snapped. He exploded, surging within her.

Shudders of pleasure racked their conjoined bodies. Lightning, thunder, fireworks, and a twenty-one-gun salute all rolled into one. Better than sex, people said, describing everything from movies to chocolate mousse. Ha! Poor fools didn't know what the hell they were talking about.

"Dixon?" Alexandra said sometime later.

He forced his eyelids open. She stared at him, her expression serious.

"What?" A prickle of alarm raced down his spine.

"I'm scared."

He tightened his arms around her. "No need to be, sweetheart. You're safe here. Nobody knows where we are. Not even Cesar. No way for the bad guys to trace us."

She shook her head slightly. "I wasn't thinking about whoever's after me. I meant . . ." Her eyelashes fanned cheeks that were tinged a delicate pink. She pressed her lips together, then tried again. "I've never felt this way before. With Mark . . ."

Dixon tensed. "Forget Mark."

She frowned. "I already have. And that's part of what scares me. A couple of days ago I was engaged to Mark. Yet here I am making love with you. This feels like the real thing, but what if . . ."

"It's a rebound thing?" He brushed the hair back off her forehead.

"Or a reaction to the danger I'm in?" She shivered slightly and burrowed into him. "You make me feel safe, Dixon."

He raised an eyebrow. "And this is a bad thing?" He touched her mouth. Her lips trembled against his fingertips.

"No." Alexandra turned away, then stood up and began pulling her clothes on. "But . . ." She shrugged.

Tell her the truth, stupid. Tell her she's more than a client. Tell her you love her. Instead, he got dressed himself. The silence crackled with the intensity of all that lay unsaid between them. But dammit, even if he found exactly the right words, she wasn't ready to listen. Despite what she might think, she still had a few issues to resolve. Jordan had weighed her down with a ton of emotional baggage.

"But what?" he asked softly. "Mark?"

"No!" She yanked the turtleneck over her head. "Mark doesn't factor into this equation."

Dixon snagged her hand and tugged her down on the sofa beside him. "Doesn't he? Tell me about Mark. You and Mark." He didn't want to hear, but he knew she needed the closure.

She stared moodily out the window at the falling snow, silent for so long, he thought she'd forgotten the question. Finally: "When we first met, Mark was so charming, so handsome, so attentive. He swept me off my feet like a fairy-tale prince."

Yeah, the guy was a real prince all right. Dixon wrapped an arm around her shoulders as if his touch could shield her from the pain he saw in her face.

She settled into him with a sigh. "Gradually, so slowly I hardly realized it was happening, he changed. He became preoccupied with his job. Or so I thought. I didn't see as much of him as I had before, and when we did go out, it was usually connected somehow to the firm, dinners with clients, socializing with his colleagues. He was still handsome, of course, and charming enough when he felt like it, but his attentiveness took the form of criticism. One time he'd say I wasn't friendly enough with a client's wife. The next time he'd say I was too friendly. Or he'd say my eye makeup made me look like an owl, my lipstick left smudges on his collar, my clothes were too conservative. When I insisted on attending my mother's fiftieth birthday party instead of accompanying him on a ski weekend with the Loomises, you'd have thought I'd committed a capital crime." She paused, out of breath.

"But the way he reacted to the threats against my life broke my heart. If he had truly cared about me, he wouldn't have ignored my worries. He proved what I'd suspected for a long time. Prince Charming was just a disguise. Mark was a frog all along." She looked at him. "You're not a frog, are you?"

His smile was rueful. "No, sweetheart, but I'm no Prince Charming either. I'm just a man who cares for you very much."

She cupped his jaw with her hand. His throat tightened at the expression on her face. "Guess I'll just have to take a chance, huh?" Very gently she touched her lips to his.

Dixon walked into the room just as Alex hung up the phone. His eyebrows slammed together in a frown. "Jordan again? What is that? The fourth time he's called?"

"The fifth. Apparently, he can't take no for an answer." Alex was so frustrated, she didn't know whether to laugh or cry.

"I'll fix his wagon." Dixon unplugged the phone. "Let him argue with a busy signal."

Why hadn't she thought of that? Such a simple solution.

Dixon laid a hand on her shoulder. "Hell of a way to spend the holidays, huh?"

Alex looked around at Great-grandmother Yano's snug little house, then up at Dixon. "I don't know. It's not so bad. I think we need a Christmas tree, though. Can't we slip into town and get one?" She crossed to the sofa and curled up at one end. Wynonna immediately wrapped herself around Alex's shoulders like a fur stole.

Dixon nudged Reba aside to claim his fair share of the rocker. "It's been snowing steadily for the last twelve hours. My four-wheel drive's pretty reliable on bad roads, but even *it* would get stuck if we tried to go anywhere. The snow is deeper than the axles and just the right temperature to pack."

"How about an artificial tree, then? Does Great-grandmother Yano have a fake Christmas tree in storage? I'd even settle for one of those ugly old aluminum ones."

"Sorry. Great-grandmother Yano's a Buddhist."

"Well, phooey!"

"Hey, it's a perfectly respectable religion."

"I didn't mean that." She looked at him sideways. "Are you Buddhist?"

"My father is."

"And your mother?"

"Lutheran."

"Which makes you . . ."

"Confused." He grinned. "Midnight services every Christmas Eve. Obon festival every summer. How about you?"

"Presbyterian, more or less." She made a face. "Actually, more less than more. We used to attend church every Sunday, but after Daddy died, we got out of the habit."

A melancholy silence fell between them. Alex didn't know what Dixon was thinking about, but her own mind was filled with memories of her father. Stuart Roundtree had been dead almost ten years now, but the grief still invaded her thoughts from time to time. Little things triggered it—certain smells she associated with her father, particular phrases he'd used, or sometimes just the time of year.

"Daddy loved Christmas," she said softly. "All of it. He used to take us up into the mountains to cut our own tree."

Dixon cleared his throat. "There aren't any trees within hiking distance, but we could cut a sagebrush."

"Really?" Alex sat up so abruptly that she dislodged the calico perched on her shoulders.

Wynonna landed awkwardly on the arm of the sofa with a disgruntled meow. Then, as if she'd planned the whole maneuver herself, she jumped down onto the floor, where she proceeded to give herself a spit bath.

"In lieu of a real Christmas tree," Dixon explained.

Alex grinned. Granted a sagebrush wasn't quite the same as a pine, but Dixon's enthusiasm was contagious. Unfortunately . . . "I don't have any warm clothes. In fact, I don't have any clothes at all other than the few things Mother bought at the mall before we left town."

"No problem. Great-grandmother left all her cold-weather gear. She doesn't need it down at Uncle Taro's."

Alex had a sudden mental image of herself in a pair of the doll-sized woman's ski pants. With any luck they might come to her knees.

She met Dixon's gaze with a skeptical expression and they both burst out laughing.

"Or maybe not," he amended. "So scratch that suggestion. Do you have any ideas?"

"Why don't we make cookies?"

"You mean like Oreos?"

Alex gave him a disgusted look. "No, not like Oreos. I'm talking real cookies. Homemade gingerbread men."

"Okay. I'm game as long as I get to eat the finished product." Dixon stood up, depriving Reba of his lap.

The cat's glare was full of reproach. She stalked off toward the kitchen, where she immediately began crunching her way through a bowl of Meow Mix.

"Darn." Alex made a face.

"What?"

"I forgot. I can't make cookies without a recipe. Maybe your great-grandmother has a cookbook?" she said hopefully.

"I doubt it. Great-grandmother's from the old school. I don't think she uses recipes."

Alex snapped her fingers. "I've got it. I'll call Mother for her recipe. She'd probably like to hear from me anyway. She worries." She jumped up, narrowly missing Wynonna's tail, then quickly sat down again. "Rats. I just remembered."

"What? The recipe?"

"No. Like Mark, Mother has caller ID. If I phone her, she'll know where we are. Not that she'd tell anyone on purpose, but . . ." She shrugged.

"The phone's in Great-grandmother's name. Even if it occurs to your mother to look Great-grandmother up in the telephone directory—"

"Believe me, she'll look. Mother doesn't miss a trick."

"Doesn't matter. She can look all she wants; she still won't be any the wiser. No address is listed."

Alex laughed. "Like that would faze Regina Roundtree. The woman has contacts all over town. If anyone knows where your great-grandmother lives, Mother will obtain that information. You can bet on it."

Dixon smiled. "You worry too much, Alexandra. Even if she knew our exact location, she'd have one hell of a time finding us. The roads aren't marked and this snow's an added complication. I think we're safe."

The illusion of safety lasted just over four hours.

At first Alex thought the buzzing sound was Dixon cutting down a sagebrush "tree" with the chain saw he'd found in the shed. By the time she realized what it really was, the snowmobile had circled the house twice. Terrified, she dropped the gingerbread man she was decorating. Her heart raced, but time itself seemed to crawl. In slow motion the cookie hit the edge of the counter, then arced toward the floor, where it bounced once, scattering crumbs across the spotless white tiles before coming to rest frosted side down.

Panic sent her rushing from door to door to check the locks, even though she knew all was secure. "Deep breaths," she muttered, positioning herself off to the side of one of the long, narrow front windows at an angle where she could peer outside without being seen.

As if on cue, the snowmobile came flying around the corner of the house, throwing up a rooster tail of snow. The driver's body was disguised by the muffling thickness of his insulated suit, his face hidden by a fake beard and sunglasses. An oversized Santa hat concealed his hair completely. The anonymous figure could have been anyone from Arnold Schwarzenegger to Madonna, anyone from Danny Hall . . . to her mother.

The snowmobiling Santa cut between two of the shrubs edging the yard, spun a quarter turn, and headed straight for the front door. Alex winced, preparing for a crash of splintering wood that never came. At the last second the big Polaris veered off to the right. Moments later Alex saw why. Dixon, his face hidden by a ski mask, came racing into her line of vision, brandishing a roaring chain saw like the villain in a cheap horror film.

Santa turned so abruptly he nearly lost control, then revved his engine one last time before fleeing back down the road in the direction of town.

Alex slumped against the wall. Her legs felt rubbery. She pressed a trembling hand to her chest. If she hadn't known better she'd have sworn someone was playing racquetball inside her rib cage.

The roar of the chain saw stopped suddenly and the silence was deafening. She fumbled with the dead bolt, clumsy in her haste. It gave way at last and she fell back to let Dixon in.

"Either Mark or my mother must have told someone where we were." She felt as if she were strangling on the words.

"Call them," snapped Dixon.

"What would Mark have to gain from terrorizing me?"

"Call him. If he's not there . . ."

Moving like a sleepwalker, Alex stumbled to the kitchen, where Reba was nibbling tentatively at the fallen gingerbread man. Up on the counter, Dolly was sampling the contents of the frosting bowl. Dixon shooed the cat away and handed Alex the phone.

She tried Mark's work number first, then home, but reached answering machines both places. She left no messages. What was there to say? Done any snowmobiling lately?

Her stomach rolled as if the cookies she'd sampled were about to turn on her. "Dead end." She hung up the receiver, then searched Dixon's expressionless face for a clue as to what he was thinking. "Okay, Mark's a pig, but I can't believe he'd do something like this."

Dixon's face remained locked in neutral. "Maybe he did. Maybe he didn't. Call your mother."

Bile rose in her throat. "My mother? You don't suspect my mother, do you?" *I don't suspect my mother, do I?*

Dixon tossed hat and gloves on a kitchen chair. "It's my job to suspect everyone."

Alex felt numb. "It can't be Mother. She only kills people in books, not real life."

He placed a hand on her shoulder. "Maybe so, but

someone out there favors a more direct approach. Call her."

Dixon stared at the mess on the kitchen floor, frowning fiercely as he tried to make sense of what he knew. Dammit, that snowmobiler could have been almost anyone. Jordan could be the guilty party or he could have quite innocently passed Great-grandmother's number out to someone else who'd traced them here.

Regina Roundtree was definitely off the hook. Alexandra was on the phone with her mother right now. But God only knew whom she'd shared information with. He tapped Alexandra's shoulder. "Ask your mother if she gave this number out to anyone."

Alexandra nodded. ". . . yes, that's right. We're staying at Dixon's great-grandmother's house." She sighed. "I knew you'd figure it out. No, I realize you wouldn't purposely put me in danger. But this is very important. Did you mention our whereabouts to anyone? Anyone at all?"

There was a short pause. Then Alexandra covered the receiver with her palm and whispered, "She says she didn't tell anyone where I was, but she did give the number out to a couple of people."

"Who?" Dixon's gut clenched.

"Mandy, for one. She said she needed to talk to me about the fire insurance on the shop."

Amanda Roundtree Sutton had a strong motive—money—but Dixon wasn't sure she had the killer instinct. "Who else?"

Alexandra's expression told him he wasn't going to like what she had to say. "Officer Rios."

The words dropped into a pool of silence, the only sounds in the kitchen the soft vibration of the refrigerator's motor and his own harsh breathing. Cesar? Hell, no! It couldn't be. What possible motive would Cesar have? Dixon felt as if a heavyweight contender had just landed a shot to his jaw, effectively scrambling his brains.

"Anything else you want to know?" Alexandra's voice brought him back to the present.

"Yeah. Ask her when she talked to them."

"When did you talk to them, Mother?"

Another pause while Alexandra absorbed her mother's reply.

"Hang on a minute," she said at length. "I need to fill Dixon in." Once again she covered the mouthpiece. "They both left messages on her machine. Mother normally won't leave the computer to talk to someone unless it's urgent. Otherwise she wouldn't get any work done," Alexandra explained. "Anyway, she wound up the chapter she was working on a couple hours ago and that's when she listened to her messages and returned calls."

"A couple hours ago," Dixon repeated, his mind racing.

"She claims she didn't tell either one of them where we were, just gave them the number where we could be reached. It doesn't necessarily have to be one of them," she argued. "Maybe they told someone else."

"Maybe."

Alexandra removed her hand from the mouthpiece. "Mother, I've got to go. Try not to worry. Dixon won't let anything happen to me." She hung up slowly. "I'm sorry. I never should have called Mother. I knew she had caller ID and I knew she couldn't keep her mouth shut." Alexandra refused to look at him.

Dixon pulled her into his arms, pressing a kiss to her forehead. "It's not your fault . . . or your mother's either. I was the one who assured you it was okay to call her."

She nestled against him, wrapping her arms around his waist. "It *is* going to be all right, isn't it?"

"Yeah," he said, hoping it was true. Though he was damned if he knew where to hide her now.

Her body tensed at the sudden shrilling of the phone.

"I'll get it." He reached across her for the receiver. "Yeah?"

"Dixon? Is that you?"

A chill snaked down his spine as he recognized the voice. "Cesar?"

"Hey, man. I been trying to reach you ever since I went off shift. Who you been on the phone with, buddy?"

"How'd you know where I was?"

"My mother—" started Alexandra.

Dixon shushed her. He wanted to hear what Cesar had to say.

"I spent half the damn day trying to trace you. I finally sweet-talked this number out of your client's mother."

"What's so urgent?"

"We found a corpse in the rubble of Gemini Gifts."

"Alexandra's mother didn't mention it."

"No way she would have known. We haven't released the information to the press."

"Have you ID'ed the body?"

"Yeah. It's Myron Finney, the bum who hung around the downtown area."

"Damn."

"We thought at first he died of smoke inhalation. He was curled up in a pile of rags in the corner behind the furnace like he'd been sleeping down there. Latch was broken on one of the side windows. We figure he must have gotten in that way."

"What is it? What body?" Alexandra demanded.

Dixon gave her shoulders a reassuring squeeze. "You said at first you thought he died of smoke inhalation. You mean he didn't?"

"Who died?" Alexandra was trembling.

"Just a minute, Cesar." He covered the mouthpiece. "The bum from the alley," he told Alexandra. "Cops found his body in the basement after the fire."

"Oh, my God."

"Okay, Cesar. What's the word?"

"Coroner says the guy was shot point-blank right in the heart. Figures he was dead a good six to ten hours before the fire."

"Damn, how'd your guys miss something as obvious as a bullet through the heart?"

"Get real, Yano. The old man's clothes were filthy. He stank to high heaven. Sergeant Kirkwood made us wear gloves just to handle the body. You think anybody was going to notice one extra hole in all those layers of rags during a casual examination? Hell, we thought he'd died of the smoke."

"He must have seen something."

"Or somebody."

Like Santa without his fake beard.

"How did the fire start?"

"The investigators haven't filed a formal report yet."

"But?"

"But the word is, they're saying arson. Fire apparently began in the supply cupboard under the stairs." Cesar cleared his throat. "I just thought you'd want to know. Stay in touch, man. And the next time you decide to take off, at least leave a number where you can be reached."

"Don't leave town, right?"

"Something like that."

"Cesar?"

"Yeah, man?"

"We're leaving in the morning."

Cesar spat out a few choice words in Spanish. "Why?"

"It's not safe here any longer."

"What are you talking about?"

"Right before you called, we had an uninvited guest. Santa on a snowmobile."

This time Cesar swore so loudly that Dixon had to hold the receiver away from his ear.

"My sentiments exactly." His tone was dry.

"Where you gonna take her?"

"I haven't decided yet."

"Well, keep in touch, man."

Dixon didn't answer. His gut told him that everything Cesar'd said was on the level, but a few niggling doubts remained. Trust no one. He should have followed that advice in the first place.

He hung up, then turned his full attention on Alexandra. "I think Cesar's trustworthy. We're friends. I've known him for years. But I don't want to take any chances. We'll leave tomorrow morning at first light."

"Why not now?" Her voice shook uncontrollably.

Dixon held her close, pressing a kiss to the top of her head. She smelled of ginger and cinnamon. "It's getting dark. There's a tractor with a blade out in the shed. I can use it to clear the road, but not until morning. The headlights don't work." He caressed her back and shoulders with slow, soothing strokes. "Don't worry. We're okay for now. I have a gun. The bastard knows a fake beard isn't going to protect him from a bullet."

"So what you're really saying is we're trapped."

He frowned. "We could walk out, but I honestly think we're safer here." He leaned back so he could examine her face, disturbed to see the tears trickling silently down her cheeks. "Do you want something to eat? It's past dinnertime."

"I'm not hungry. Just upset. Why would anyone want to hurt that harmless old bum? Earlier this week—God, was it only the day before yesterday?—I saw him rummaging through the trash bin behind the store. He looked so cold and miserable, I gave him the leftover muffins and fudge from the break room." She shuddered. "And now he's dead. It doesn't make sense. None of this makes sense." Her voice rose, approaching hysteria.

Dixon folded her close. "Hang in there, sweetheart. The cops will get to the bottom of the mystery; that's their job. And I'll keep you safe; that's my job."

A strong sense of déjà vu assailed Alex a few minutes past two as she slipped into the bedroom where Dixon was sleeping. Though this time, she promised herself, there was no question of telephonis interruptus. She'd taken Mandy's advice and unplugged the phone.

Of course, there was one other major difference. She wasn't wearing pale silk this time. After her shower, she'd changed into one of Great-grandmother Yano's high-necked flannel nightgowns. The voluminous purple-and-orange plaid garment boasted long sleeves that hit her just below the elbow, a hem that covered her knees, and yards of fabric that masked any hint of a curve in between. Victoria's Secret, it was not.

"Dixon?" she whispered. "Are you awake?"

He sat up immediately, reaching for his gun. "What's wrong?"

"I'm cold and stiff. Naomi and Wynonna are hogging the pillows and Dolly and Reba stole all my covers."

"Those cats are spoiled rotten."

"May I sleep in here with you?" Actually, sleep wasn't exactly what she had in mind.

"On one condition."

"Another condition?" What was it with him and his conditions?

"Just one. Lose the nightgown. That material's so loud, it'd keep me up all night."

She smiled. Keeping him up all night was pretty much the idea. "But it's cold."

"I'll keep you warm."

Hot was more like it. Still smiling, she tugged the offending garment off over her head an inch at a time and dropped it in a pile on the floor. She wasn't wearing anything underneath. "How's that? Better?"

Their gazes locked with a jolt, the expression on Dixon's face triggering little charges of excitement in all her major erogenous zones.

"Oh, yeah." He lifted the covers to welcome her in and she realized he was as naked as she was.

She slid into his arms, her body locking in place as snugly as a Lego piece.

"Hey," he protested as she pressed a string of kisses

along his collarbone, "I thought you asked if you could *sleep* with me."

"Sleep? In your dreams maybe." She whispered the words against his throat, one hand burying itself in the hair at the nape of his neck while the other snaked down between their bodies to reach for him. He was rock hard before she started on the second collarbone.

"Can I play too?"

"I thought you were sleepy." She wriggled up to nip at his lower lip.

"Not me. Sleep's the furthest thing from my mind."

"Really?" She gave him one last, lingering squeeze, then eased her body away from his and marched her fingers up his abdomen and across his chest. "If sleep's the furthest thing from your mind, then what's the nearest thing?"

"Witch." Dixon's eyes gleamed in the moonlight streaming through the slats of the blinds. "This," he said, pulling her hips hard against him. "And this." He massaged her nipples with a finesse that nearly toppled her right over the edge. "And this." Dixon's kiss short-circuited her few remaining brain cells.

She couldn't think. She couldn't breathe. She dragged her mouth from his, gasping for air. "Oh, God. Dixon." She quivered uncontrollably, the tension in her body unbearable. Instinctively, she reached for him. "I want you. I want you now."

Dixon grabbed her wrists, then forced her onto her back, both arms pinned above her head. "Patience is a virtue."

ELEVEN

His kiss was leisurely.

Alexandra shuddered and arched her back, straining to rub herself against him.

When he touched the sensitive spot at the juncture of her thighs, she stilled for a moment. Her eyes looked huge and luminous. "Dixon, please!"

He slipped two fingers inside. She was slick and ready.

"Oh, God. Oh, God."

He entered her in one smooth movement.

She rocked her pelvis upward in welcome. "Yes," she said. "Yes!"

And the world exploded in a wild eruption of pleasurable sensation.

"I love you," she whispered long after the last of the violent paroxysms had subsided, when Dixon lay drowsing in that no-man's-land that lay between waking and sleeping.

Or maybe not. Perhaps what he heard was no more than the echo of his own heart.

"What was that?" Alexandra reared up in bed. Moonlight poured through the opened slats of the blinds to paint her body in silver-blue stripes.

"I didn't hear anything. I think you were dreaming." Dixon put his hand on her shoulder; she was vibrating with tension.

"No, I heard something. I'm sure of it."

"Okay." He gave her shoulder a squeeze. "In that case, I'd better check it out." He pulled on his jeans and boots, then grabbed his gun from the table by the bed. "You stay here. I'll be right back."

Alexandra caught his arm. Her eyes looked huge. "Watch your step, Dixon."

He crept through the darkened house, making his way to the front windows overlooking the drive. He pulled the drapes open a crack and peered out. Nothing moved outside. No fresh tracks marred the perfection of the snowy drifts. He listened intently, but all he heard was the whine of a chinook wind and the steady drip of water melting off the roof.

Suddenly a three-foot strip of icicles fell from the eaves with a clatter.

"Did you hear that?" Alexandra called from the bedroom.

Dixon smiled to himself in the darkness. "Nothing to worry about," he yelled. "Just icicles parting company with the roof."

Alexandra emerged from the bedroom. "Thank God. Sorry I was so jumpy."

"Better safe than sorry." Dixon uttered the cliché absently. He hadn't counted on the wind. If the snow kept melting like this, they wouldn't stay isolated for long.

He stared out at the full moon reflecting off the snow. It wasn't daylight, but he could see—even without headlights. Maybe he ought to get the tractor started and the road plowed. The sooner they moved on, the better.

"Dixon?" Alexandra hugged Great-grandmother Yano's ugly olive-green comforter around herself for warmth. "What are you doing?"

"Thinking. Bad habit of mine."

"Thinking about what?"

"About how long it's going to take this wind to melt all the snow."

She shivered. "But if the snow melts . . ."

"Exactly. I'm going to get dressed, then go out and see if I can get the old John Deere started."

"I'll pack." Her voice was soft, but full of determination. Dixon was proud of her.

"Throw in some food while you're at it."

"Why? Where are we going?"

"It's time for last resorts."

A rustic sign hung suspended between two colorful, rough-hewn totem poles. "The Last Resort," Alex read aloud. "I didn't realize you were being quite so literal."

"I know the owner. It's not really a resort, just a glorified bed-and-breakfast that caters to the yuppie trade, but Kurt has big plans. He's a mover and shaker. Even my mother considers him a model of success, despite the fact he rarely wears a tie." Dixon glanced down at his watch. "Nine-twenty. With any luck, the breakfast buffet's still set out. I don't know about you, but I'm starving."

"After scarfing down half a box of crackers?"

Dixon's grin made her heart do a flip-flop. "I'm a big boy, Alexandra. It takes a lot to fill me up."

Dixon was a man who'd stand out in any crowd, but at the moment, with his rumpled clothing, bloodshot eyes, and heavy-duty stubble, Alex feared he would stand out for all the wrong reasons. Even to her, partial as she was, he looked like a thug, and she suspected she didn't look much better.

"I *am* hungry, but the last thing I want to do is call attention to myself, and as disheveled as I am right now . . ." She let it trail off. Maybe she was being overly cautious.

"Damn. I hadn't thought of that." Dixon rubbed a hand across his bristly jaw. "I probably look more like an escaped convict than a paying guest myself."

He drove the Jeep around the back of the lodge, past the converted machinery shed designated for guest parking, and parked in a smaller, three-bay garage. The Jeep—nestled between a vintage Cadillac, glossy black and heavy with chrome, and a red '65 'Vette in mint condition—was as out of place as she and Dixon were. "Kurt's a collector," Dixon said. "Or anyway, a temporary collector."

"Meaning?" Alex got out of the Jeep, careful not to bang her door into the Corvette.

"He buys them, restores them, then sells them and starts all over again. I've never known him to keep the same car longer than a couple years."

She stroked the Corvette's shiny crimson hood. "How can he bear to part with them?"

Dixon smiled. "For Kurt, the pleasure's in the transformation, not the ownership."

Alex turned as one of the big doors rolled up. The man standing there was tall, lanky, and loose-limbed, with long, fair hair, heavy-lidded pale blue eyes, and a droopy mustache.

"Guest parking's over there, miss." Yawning, he indicated the direction with a languid wave of his hand.

Dixon stepped forward. "Kurt, old buddy. You don't expect me to park with the hoi polloi, do you?"

When he caught sight of Dixon, Kurt's eyes brightened and his mustache twitched. Alex suspected the lips hidden underneath were stretched in a smile.

"Get outta here, Dix."

The men wrung each other's hands and slapped each other's shoulders in a ritual Alex thought looked more like the opening round of a fight than a friendly greeting.

"How you doin', you old horse thief?"

"Just fine, Yano. Better than you are anyway, from the looks of you. What's going on? You haven't traded the PI biz for a life of crime, I hope. You look like you're on the run."

"We are, in a manner of speaking. I probably should have called first, but we were a little rushed." He introduced Alex, then explained their situation in a few stark sentences that somehow made the events of the past few days sound all the more terrifying.

Kurt propped himself against the Jeep's rear bumper. "I take it you need a place to hole up for a while."

A muscle twitched beneath Dixon's eye. "Right."

"*Mi casa es su casa.* I have a couple empty rooms on

the second floor and one dormer room on the third. Take your pick."

"How about the apartment here?"

"Over the garage?" Kurt's nose wrinkled in distaste. "It's not very fancy. I don't rent it out except to college kids during the height of the ski season. Nobody's using it now. If that's what you want . . ." He shrugged. "Be my guest. We won't be busy enough to need it again until Anthony Lakes opens all their runs. Season's running late. They don't have a heavy enough base yet. Do you ski?" he asked Alex.

"Yes," she murmured, suddenly reminded of all the ski weekends she and Mark had spent cozily ensconced in B&Bs much like this one.

Kurt snorted. "Then you'll have to teach Dix. He's never progressed beyond the bunny hill."

"I have other skills." Dixon shot her a private look.

Alex's cheeks burned. Indeed he did.

Kurt glanced from Dixon to Alex, then back to Dixon. "You sure you don't want the dormer room? It has its own Jacuzzi."

Dixon shook his head regretfully. "The garage apartment's more private."

"Bunk beds and a shower, no tub."

"We'll manage."

Dixon's offhand assurance sent a series of erotic pictures rushing through her head. Damn her overactive imagination. Alex fought to keep her expression neutral.

"Okay. Whatever suits you tickles me plumb to death, as my uncle Tex used to say." Kurt handed Dixon a key. "Are you two hungry?"

"Starving. We haven't eaten since dinner last night

and neither one of us has had more than a couple hours' sleep."

"I'll bring something over in about fifteen minutes, okay? You're in luck. Ginger made quiche this morning."

"Ginger Ellingson is Kurt's partner," Dixon explained.

"Ginger Ellingson," she repeated. She turned to Kurt. "I don't believe I caught your last name."

The mustache twitched again, even more violently this time. "Swenson. Kurt Swenson. Yano and I are first cousins."

"My compliments to the cook." Alex gave a sigh of contentment. It was a wonder the difference a shower and a good, hot meal could make.

"I'll be sure to pass them along to Ginger." Kurt turned to Dixon, who looked at least fifty percent better since he'd shaved. "Anything else I can get you?"

"No. You've done enough."

Kurt lounged against the door frame. "Got any plans?"

Alex spoke up. "I need some clothes. I lost virtually every stitch I owned in the fire."

"Can't help you there. Neither Ginger nor I is the right size. Closest shopping would be in Baker City. Dix knows the way."

"And I've got some calls to make," Dixon added.

"Help yourself. Phone's on the wall over there."

Dixon shook his head. "No, I'll make my calls from a pay phone. I don't want to be traced." He and Alex exchanged a look.

"Whatever you think is best." Kurt shrugged. "Oh,

and before I forget, Ginger invited both of you to dinner tonight. You're not a vegetarian, are you, Alexandra?"

"No."

"Good. Ginger is planning to try out a new chicken recipe for the Friday-night buffet. You two can be the guinea pigs."

Alex smiled. "I like surprises."

"I don't," Dixon growled. "What's wrong with steak and potatoes?"

"Cholesterol, cuz. Ginger says we should be careful at our age."

"Nothing wrong with my arteries."

Kurt raised an eyebrow. "Still living on cold cereal and fast food, I presume?"

"I cook."

"Yeah, what? Hot dogs? Frozen pizza?"

"And pot pies. Ramen noodles."

Kurt made a face. "Salt, fat, and preservatives. I rest my case."

Dixon turned Alexandra and her mother's charge cards—her own had burned in the fire—loose on the dress shops of downtown Baker City while he filled the Jeep's gas tank and made a few necessary phone calls.

The first was simple enough, a brief message left on the answering machine at his father's office. He detailed the circumstances that had resulted in his cutting short his house-sitting stint and requested that the senior Yano arrange for someone else to look after Great-grand-mother's cats.

He reached a machine on the second call too. This time his message was even shorter. Without giving any details, he told Regina Roundtree that her daughter was safe and staying at an unidentified location. He hung up quickly, half-afraid she might pick up and demand all the details. Having endured one of her marathon interviews last summer, Dixon knew his discretion was no match for Regina's curiosity.

An actual human voice answered the third call. "Brunswick Police Department." The dispatcher connected him with Cesar.

"Man, where are you?"

"I'd rather not say. We're running out of places to hide."

"Who knew you two were at your great-granny's place?"

"Short list. Aside from a few members of my family who are probably no longer on speaking terms with me, just Alex's mother, her sister, Mark Jordan, and you."

"Either one of the Roundtrees have a motive?"

"Damn it all, everyone connected with the case has a motive."

"What about the fiancé?"

"Former fiancé," Dixon said quickly.

"Oh, yeah? You don't say? Way to go, man."

"It's not like that."

"Oh, yeah? Then tell me, what is it like? What's *she* like?"

"You're disgusting, Rios."

Cesar laughed at the crude course of action Dixon advised. "Hey, man. I'm flexible, but not *that* flexible."

Dixon grunted.

"Seriously, Dix, what about Jordan? Maybe he's holding a grudge."

"I'd like to believe he was guilty. The creep turns my

stomach. He cheated on his wife and he cheated on Alexandra. Does having the morals of an alley cat automatically qualify him as the prime suspect? I don't know." He fell silent a moment. "It wasn't you, was it?"

"What do you think?" Cesar's voice was strained.

"Sorry. I had to ask."

"Yeah, I suppose you did, but you should damn well know better than to suspect me. I'm a cop, one of the good guys."

"I'm getting paranoid. Got anything new on Danny Hall?"

"No, but while I'm at it maybe I'll haul the scuzzbag in and lean on him, see what he has to say for himself." Cesar paused. "Listen, man, is there a number where you can be reached or someplace I could leave a message? How about your cell phone?"

"No!" The word came out a little more emphatically than Dixon had planned. He took a deep breath. Trust no one, he reminded himself. "My phone burned up in the fire. Don't worry. I'll check in with you tomorrow. You can tell me then what you've come up with."

"I'm off this weekend. You'll have to contact me at home."

"You planning to be around?"

Cesar chuckled. "You know me so well. Call before six."

"Hot date?"

"Sizzling."

"This one's not married to a Neanderthal truck driver, is she?"

"God, I hope not." A trace of apprehension entered Cesar's voice. "I forgot to ask."

"Some guys never learn."

❖————————————❖

Ginger's red hair hadn't surprised Alex, but his gender had. "Kurt's partner is quite a cook. If I stay around here for long, I'm going to weigh two hundred pounds." Keeping an eye on Dixon, she curled up at one end of the sofa in the garage apartment.

He stood staring out the window at the falling snow, a puzzled frown creasing his brow.

"Is something wrong?"

"What?" He turned to face her. "Yeah, something's wrong, but the hell of it is I don't know what." He shook his head slowly from side to side. "No matter how I shuffle the puzzle pieces, they just don't fit. Alexandra, is there anyone we've forgotten? Anyone else who stands to benefit from your death? Anyone else who has a motive, no matter how slim?"

She caught her lower lip between her teeth. "I've been racking my brains, but I can't think of a soul." Someone wanted her dead, but who could possibly hate her that much?

"Do you want to ride into Baker City with me?" he asked abruptly.

"Are you kidding? It's almost midnight. And it's snowing."

"I'll chain up and drive slowly."

"But why so late? What can you do in Baker City that you can't do here?"

His expression was grim. "Use a pay phone. I want to talk to Cesar, find out what he learned today."

"Can't it wait until tomorrow?" She stifled a yawn.

"I'm probably going off half-cocked here, but dammit, Alexandra, I have this sick feeling in my gut. What if

Cesar discovered something crucial this afternoon? Something that blows the case wide open? Only he can't warn us because he has no way to track us down."

She pulled on her new snow boots and began searching for her mittens, despite the fact that going out in the storm was far down on her own list of priorities, "Do the wild thing with Dixon" being first on the list, followed immediately by "Get ten solid hours of sleep." Oh, well. The sooner he put his mind to rest, the sooner they could move on to her agenda.

"What are you waiting for, Dixon? Christmas? Let's go."

His smile warmed her clear to her toes. Who needed thermal underwear and electric socks?

"Cesar?"

The answering grunt was marginally human, definitely testy.

"Cesar?"

"Dammit, Dix, is that you? Why the hell are you calling this time of night?"

"It's only one."

"One there maybe, but two here, moron. Dammit, where are you?"

Dixon ignored the question.

"Why'd you call? Has something happened to Ms. Roundtree?"

"No, she's fine. In fact, she's right here with me, crammed into this phone booth." *Distracting the hell out of me.* Though he didn't share that information with Cesar. "I called because I wanted to know what you found out this afternoon."

"Hell, man. When do you sleep?" Cesar didn't wait for an answer. He did a little more cussing, in Spanish this time. "Can't find my damn case notes. Oh, here they are. Look, I don't know if any of this will help, but here goes. I pulled Danny Hall in for questioning. Had a hell of a time running him down. Talked to the Calzacorta woman at work—she's a checker at Albertson's—and she told me Hall was at her place baby-sitting, if you can believe it. When I showed up, he and the Calzacorta kids were all sitting around the kitchen table gluing wiggle eyes, red felt noses, and pipe-cleaner antlers on candy canes."

"Whoa. Hold it. Did you say Wendy Calzacorta worked at Albertson's?" Beside him, Alexandra stiffened.

"Right. So?"

"So some checker at Albertson's has been giving Alexandra the evil eye for the past couple months."

"Hall probably painted her as Public Enemy Number One. Ask your client what her evil-eyed checker looks like."

Dixon passed along Cesar's request.

Alexandra shivered. "Medium. Medium height. Medium weight. Medium coloring."

"Medium—" started Dixon.

"Yeah, I heard. Does she have frizzy hair? Glasses?"

"Frizzy hair?" Dixon repeated. "Glasses?"

Alexandra nodded.

"Yes to both," he told Cesar.

"Well, that clears up one little mystery."

"What did Hall have to say for himself?"

"Claimed he didn't know what the hell I was getting at."

"You believe him?"

"Hell, who knows? Guys like that spend so much time lying, they sound more believable when they're spinning some yarn than they do when they're telling the gospel truth."

"Anything else?"

"Nah. I tried to get ahold of Jordan this afternoon, but all I could learn from that damn snooty secretary of his was that he'd left town for the holiday. Skiing, she thought—which was probably the truth since he didn't answer his phone at home. I tried several times this afternoon and then again this evening."

"Damn handful of nothing," Dixon muttered. "That it?"

"The whole enchilada. Now, can I get back to sleep?"

"Sure. Thanks, buddy." Dixon hung up, more depressed now than he had been earlier. He leaned his forehead against the chilly glass wall of the booth.

"Dixon?" Alexandra's voice was as tentative as her touch on his arm. "What now?"

What was wrong with him? He was supposed to be taking care of her and instead he was doing his best to turn her into a human Popsicle. Her teeth were chattering and she was shivering uncontrollably.

"Why don't I see if the motel here's full?" He nodded up at the neon sign advertising the Sunridge Inn. "It's already after one, and the drive back would take at least an hour. If you don't get warm soon, you're going to end up with pneumonia."

She bared her chattering teeth in a brave smile. "Sounds like an excellent plan to me. And if you think it would help us get a room, I could always stuff my purse up under my coat so I'd look eight months pregnant."

He laughed. "I don't think that will be necessary. The vacancy sign is still lit up."

He left Alexandra waiting in the Jeep with the motor running and the heater blowing lukewarm air while he checked in.

"I hope you don't mind," he said as he took his place behind the wheel. "I paid cash for the room and signed the register as Mr. and Mrs. Joseph Carpenter."

"Clever pseudonym, Dixon, but weren't you afraid they'd say there was no room at the inn?"

He pulled around to park in front of Unit 12.

"Why use a fake name anyway? What's wrong with Mr. and Mrs. Dixon Ya—" She broke off.

"Alexandra?" He cut the engine and turned to face her.

She stared steadily at her mittened fists.

"Alexandra?" He tipped her face up to his. "It's not what you're thinking."

"How do you know what I'm thinking?"

"Your face is as transparent as glass." He rubbed the back of his hand across the softness of her cheek. "I was just being cautious. That's what you're paying me for. Trust no one. Remember?" He kissed her gently. "Now let's get inside before the desk clerk realizes we don't have any luggage."

TWELVE

"Traveling light has its advantages." Dixon slid his hands slowly up and down Alexandra's naked body.

Unit 12 was equipped with a comfortable king-size bed that Dixon had fully intended to use for sleeping until Alexandra's lack of nightwear distracted him.

"Yes." With a sigh of satisfaction, Alexandra slipped her arms around his neck and tilted her face up to his.

Never let it be said that Dixon Yano couldn't take a hint. He brushed her lips with his own, teasing them open with the tip of his tongue.

Moaning a protest at what she apparently considered his frustrating delaying tactics, Alexandra buried her hands in his hair and forced his mouth down hard on hers.

Her kisses played havoc with his senses. A fierce, hot flood of desire engulfed him, a throbbing need he felt echoed in the silky skin beneath his roving hands. Alexandra quivered under his touch.

To hell with finesse. Breathing raggedly, he rolled her onto her back.

A smile tipped the corners of her mouth. "Yes," she breathed against his lips, and spread her legs in welcome.

Dixon lost the last vestiges of control as he plunged into her silken warmth. She felt so good, so damn good. . . .

He groaned as Alexandra arched her body to meet him stroke for stroke. "Oh, God. Alexandra, you're killing me!"

"Now, Dixon. Now." She writhed wildly beneath him, gasping for breath.

Moaning deep in his throat, sobbing her name, he came fast in a wild and passionate explosion.

Sobbing and shuddering, her muscles clenching him tightly, Alexandra sank her nails in Dixon's back, her teeth in his shoulder.

"Six o'clock, Dixon. Time to be up and at 'em."

He mumbled something unintelligible and burrowed under the covers.

Alex prodded his recumbent form. "Come on, sleepyhead. Rise and shine. I'm starving to death."

He pushed aside the pillow covering his face and opened one eye. "Hungry again so soon?"

"Soon?" Alex sat up, hugging the sheet across her breasts. "I haven't eaten for hours. Not since dinner last night with Ginger and Cousin Kurt."

Dixon rolled up on one elbow and stared at her. The twinkle in his eyes belied his fierce expression. "You're forgetting that little midnight snack. You might have warned me you were a cannibal."

"What are you complaining about? I didn't even break the skin." Alex smiled slowly and seductively. "Of course, if you'd like, I'd be more than happy to kiss it and make it better."

Dixon tipped his head to one side as if he were giving her offer serious consideration. "Well . . . okay."

Alex pressed a lingering kiss to his shoulder. "Better?" she whispered in his ear.

"Oh, yeah, but . . ." Dixon leaned back against the pillow, indicating the base of his throat. "I think I've got another sore spot here."

"Poor baby." Alex pressed a kiss to the hollow of his throat, then slid her tongue up the side of his neck.

"And here." He touched his mouth.

Alex shot him a skeptical sideways glance. "Didn't Harrison Ford use this routine in *Raiders of the Lost Ark*?"

Dixon grinned. "Whatever works."

Three hours later Dixon pulled the Jeep back into the garage at the Last Resort. "I'm going to go check in with Kurt. Want to come with me?"

Smiling, Alexandra shook her head. "No, thanks. I think I'll hole up and read my way through the stack of books I bought in Baker City."

The closer they had come to the resort, the quieter Alexandra had grown. Dixon knew she was worried. He only wished he could have told her something to put her mind at rest. Unfortunately, the only news he had wasn't encouraging. During his morning phone call with Cesar he'd learned that Danny Hall had left Brunswick for parts unknown. The Calzacorta woman claimed he was on his way to California to stay with family over Christmas. If so, his appearance was going to be a big surprise because no one down there was expecting him. Cesar had checked.

So where was Hall really going? Was there any way he could have traced them? Was he lurking in the shadows somewhere, waiting for a clean shot? Planning another midnight bonfire?

Frowning, Dixon shouldered his way through the back door. The kitchen was warm and fragrant with the batch of maple sticky buns Ginger was just pulling from the big commercial oven.

"You missed breakfast," the redhead told him, "but if you can hang on a tick, you're welcome to try one of these. Coffee's in the pot. Regular, I'm afraid. The latte machine's on the fritz."

"Thanks anyway. I ate in Baker City. Where's Kurt?"

"In the main lounge playing ye olde host." Ginger winked. "He does it so well."

Except for a couple dressed for a day on the slopes, Kurt was alone in the room. Dressed in jeans, a Fair Isle sweater, and hikers, he lounged against the rustic mantelpiece, describing the best route to Anthony Lakes. Dixon noticed that Kurt's burgundy-and-blue sweater matched the decor. Knowing Kurt, the match was no coincidence.

Kurt acknowledged his entrance with the wag of one finger and a slight nod of his head. Alerted to Dixon's presence, the skiers turned. Dixon knew the look of shock on their faces was mirrored on his own. Talk about coincidence.

"Jordan?"

"Yano!" Mark Jordan made it sound like a dirty word. "What are you doing here?" His face was pasty beneath his tan. If he was faking his surprise, he was doing one hell of a job of it—a real Oscar-winning performance. He kept a nervous eye on the archway behind Dixon as if he expected Alexandra to appear at any moment. Shelby Winters clutched his arm.

Dixon eyed them both coldly. "I'd ask you the same thing, but I think it's obvious."

Kurt, ever the genial host, broke the awkward silence that followed Dixon's remark. "I take it you three know one another. Why don't I leave you alone so you can catch up on old times?"

As Kurt slipped into the adjoining room Dixon shot his cousin a dirty look. Kurt had always had a talent for avoiding awkward situations, and this particular situation promised to be about as awkward as they came.

"Where's Alex?"

Dixon's smile held little humor. "Safe."

"Damn you, Yano. I've been worried sick about her. Where do you have her hidden?"

"Worried?" Dixon laughed. "That's a joke."

"I need to talk to her. I need to explain."

"Explain what? How you can't keep your hands off other women?"

Shelby had the grace to blush, but Jordan wasn't the type to take responsibility for his own actions. His mouth narrowed to a thin line of hatred. "You did this. You poisoned her mind against me. What lies did you tell her, Yano?"

"I didn't tell her squat. How do you expect her to react? She caught you at a motel with another woman."

A spasm rippled across Shelby's face.

Jordan swore. "I can explain that! Dammit, let me

talk to her. I'll make her understand. Alex is the one I love."

"Alexandra?" Dixon raised an eyebrow. "Or Alexandra's trust fund?"

"You son of a bitch." Jordan shook off Shelby's restraining hand and advanced within inches of Dixon, murder in his eye.

"Go ahead, Jordan. Take a poke at me. I'd love an excuse to knock the teeth down your lying throat."

"Stop it. This is stupid." Shelby's voice rose shrilly. She clung to Jordan's arm, trying to pull him away from Dixon.

Jordan flicked her off as casually as a piece of lint.

The redhead stumbled backward, landing awkwardly on a burgundy leather wingback chair.

Jordan turned to Dixon, his expression venomous. "Where are you hiding her, you bastard?"

"Someplace where you'll never get your filthy hands on her."

"Who has filthy hands?" Ginger entered the room at a trot, two paper sacks in one hand and a thermos jug in the other. "You, Dix? Don't touch the furniture, then. We just had everything reupholstered and it cost the earth. Oh!" He planted himself directly between the other two men. "Here's the lunch you ordered." He pressed the food on Jordan, who was too surprised to do anything but take it. "Have a fabulous day on the slopes. They're saying the new powder up top is simply to die for."

"Come on, Mark. Fighting won't get you anywhere. You're a civilized human being. Don't stoop to his level." Shelby urged Jordan toward the door.

Dixon smirked at Jordan over Ginger's bulky shoulder. "Later."

"Outside," added the cook. "Blood is *so* difficult to remove from the carpet."

"This isn't over," Jordan blustered. "I *will* talk to Alex."

"Come on." Shelby tugged once more at his arm. This time Jordan let her lead him toward the door. Just before they left, however, Shelby surprised Dixon by turning around to face him for a second. "He does love her, you know." Her eyes were tragic, but her chin was firm.

No, he doesn't. In that moment Dixon felt sorry for her. Jordan didn't love Alexandra, but he didn't love Shelby either. He'd cheated on her just like he'd cheated on Alexandra. The sad part was, Shelby knew it and loved him all the same.

As the front door slammed behind them Dixon turned to Ginger. "An inspired entrance."

Ginger sank down on one of the two plaid sofas set at right angles to the fireplace. "Kurt's idea. I used to be a bouncer at a disco club in Portland back in the seventies." A slow, reminiscent smile spread across his homely face. "I thought for a minute there the Ken doll was going to try to punch you out."

"*Try* being the operative word."

"Well, if he *tries* again, I don't give a rat's behind if you beat him to a bloody pulp. Just make sure you do the deed out-of-doors. I wasn't kidding earlier. Blood really is hell to get out of the carpet." He glanced up as Kurt strolled in. "Did they leave?"

Kurt nodded. "Coast is clear. Sorry about that, Dix. If I had realized who the guy was, I'd have turned him

away when he showed up last night looking for a room."
He collapsed in the wing chair with a grunt.

"I told you about Jordan, warned you he might show
up."

"Yes, but Jordan didn't register with his real name."

"Oh, yeah?"

"He rented the room as John Smith. Actually, Mr.
and Mrs. John Smith."

Ginger rolled his eyes. "God, how original."

Dixon frowned. "And you didn't suspect John Smith
might be a phony name?"

"Oh, I was sure of it." Kurt stifled a yawn.

Dixon raised his eyebrows.

"We get Mr. and Mrs. John Smith an average of
twice a week," Ginger confided. "The poor deluded
fools always think they're being so clever."

"As a rule, they're couples who are married—just not
to each other."

"Damn, what a mess." Dixon could feel a headache
starting at his temples.

"Frankly, my dear boy, I think you're worried about
nothing." Ginger shook a finger for emphasis. "Jordan
might have a shot at you, but he seems genuinely attached to your Alexandra."

Dixon hit the mantel with his fist and started to protest.

"Wait," Ginger interrupted. "Let me guess. *Seems* is
the operative word."

Dixon knew damn well that Mark Jordan wasn't in
love with Alexandra. He was, however, deeply attached
to Alexandra's money, and no matter how much Dixon

wanted to pin the murder attempts on the philandering slimeball, he just couldn't convince himself Jordan was a threat. The man had no motive. Zero.

And Cousin Shelby had even less. The redhead might have the hots for Alexandra's ex-fiancé, but that hardly called for a solution as drastic as murder. And the fire had left her unemployed, a poor incentive for arson.

Yet their sudden appearance on the scene couldn't be a coincidence. They must be up to something.

Reluctantly, he mounted the steps to the garage apartment. He didn't look forward to sharing this latest development with Alexandra.

Dixon paused on the landing, then knocked out the series they'd agreed on, three quick raps, two slow, then three quick.

"Who is it?" Her voice quavered.

Smiling grimly, Dixon nodded. This was good. She was being cautious, following the rules.

"It's me. Dixon. Open up."

"What's your middle name?"

Dixon's smile faded. This wasn't part of the prearranged precautions. Something must have frightened her.

"Olaf. Olaf Kenichi."

"Oh, Dixon! Thank God!" Alexandra drew the bolt and pushed the door open. Then she threw herself on his chest, burrowing against him, hugging him tight.

"Hey, what's going on?" He held her at arm's length to study her face. Her eyes looked huge, her expression stricken. A strand of hair was stuck to her cheek. He smoothed it back behind her ear.

"Mark's here. And Shelby too. I saw them. They

drove off a few minutes ago in Mark's T-bird, but they were here. I swear it." She was shaking.

Her distress tore at his heart. Dixon pulled her close once more, soothing her with his hands, stroking her shoulders and upper arms. "It's all right. I believe you. I saw them too."

She went stiff in his embrace. "Did they see you?"

"Yes."

"No." She pulled away from him. "No, I don't believe this. Not Mark. It can't be." She paced frantically across the narrow room, her movements jerky, her eyes wide and terrified.

"Look, I don't know for sure what Jordan is doing here, but just because he's shown up, it doesn't necessarily follow that he's the villain. He's a two-timing scum, but I honestly don't think he's the one who wants you dead."

Alexandra halted her frenzied pacing. "Then why's he here?"

"For the skiing?"

"You're suggesting his presence is sheer coincidence?"

"Cesar told me yesterday that Jordan's secretary claimed he'd left town for a skiing vacation."

"Mark likes to ski the Idaho runs. I've never known him to come up here."

"Okay, say his appearance is more than coincidence. Say he traced us up here somehow. That still doesn't mean he's the one trying to kill you. Maybe all he wants to do is talk you into taking his ring back."

"Never." Alexandra hugged herself tightly. "But if it's not Mark, then it must be Shelby. She's always been jealous of Mandy and me. All through school she made a dead set for every guy we showed the slightest interest in. It was like some sick competition." She paused, her brow knit in thought. "Hating Mark was a pretense. I bet she's been after him all along."

"Or he's been after her." Dixon wished the words back as soon as he said them.

"What?" Alexandra met his gaze unflinchingly.

Time for the truth, the whole truth, and nothing but the truth. Dixon took a deep breath.

"Look, you saw him kissing his boss's wife, right? And caught him coming out of a motel room with his arm around a blonde. Face it. Mark Jordan is a world-class womanizer."

"What do you mean?"

"My first contact with him came two years ago when his wife Colleen hired me to follow him."

"You worked for his first wife? Why didn't you tell me? Why didn't you explain all this when I first tried to hire you?" Alexandra sounded as if she were strangling on the words.

"You didn't hire me to report on the state of your fiancé's morals."

Her mouth formed a tight line. "Tell me the rest of it, Dixon. I take it Mark was cheating on his wife?" She turned away from him.

Dixon could see the tension in her shoulders and the set of her head. Oh, hell. Why not just spit it all out? He was sick of keeping secrets. Who was he trying to protect anyway?

"Yes." He was careful to keep his voice even and unemotional. "I followed him for a week and quickly came to the conclusion that Jordan was cheating on his wife."

"Who was the other woman?"

"Women," he corrected. "Six different women."

She whipped around to stare at him with disbelieving eyes. "Six? *Six* different women? In a week? Who?"

"I didn't bother getting all the names. Most of them were one-night stands. Or one-afternoon stands. He did the majority of his tomcatting in the daylight hours. A brunette named Chrissie Koehler was the only one he saw more than once."

Alexandra shook her head. "I don't know her."

"She left town after the divorce. Apparently until she was named as corespondent, she had no idea Jordan was married."

"He lied to her too?"

"Obviously."

"So you've known all along what kind of man Mark was?"

"Yes."

"And you didn't bother to tell me?"

"Be reasonable, Alexandra. I couldn't tell you."

"Why not? It seems only simple decency to me. You see someone floundering around in quicksand and you throw them a rope."

"It wasn't quite like that."

"No?"

He couldn't think of anything to say.

Alexandra planted herself directly in front of him and poked his chest with her forefinger. "You must have realized he was up to his old tricks when you found Shelby's earring on my mother's bed. Why didn't you tell me the rest of it then?" She poked him again. "Answer me, dammit."

"Sweetheart—"

"Don't you sweetheart me. I trusted that bastard. I thought he was in love with me. I thought I was in love with him." Her voice broke on the last word.

Dixon tried to draw her into the comfort of his arms, but she pushed him away.

Her shoulders shook. Tears streamed down her face. She hugged herself, rocking back and forth on the balls of her feet. "How could you keep something like that a secret? Whose side are you on, anyway?"

"Confidentiality is a big part of my job, Alexandra. I didn't feel the information was mine to share. After all, you hadn't hired me to do a background check on your fiancé. You weren't paying me to keep him under surveillance."

"I never heard such a load of self-righteous drivel in my life. You withheld vital information just because I hadn't specifically asked you to search for it. Tell me, if you had accidentally discovered that my sister was cooking the books at Gemini Gifts, would you have withheld that information too?"

"Of course not. That would have been unethical."

"Oh, I see. It's unethical not to tattle when money's involved, but when it's my emotional well-being that's at stake, then it's unethical to tell. Listen to yourself, Dixon. You're not making any sense."

"Alexandra." He reached for her, thinking to calm her down, but she slapped him away and backed out of reach.

"Leave me alone, Dixon. I don't want to talk to you anymore. I need some time to think things through."

He left without another word. The bolt snapping into place behind him held a note of finality. He'd known this would happen sooner or later. He'd finally blown it big time.

Alex found Kurt in the lounge, staring into the fire with heavy-lidded eyes. He looked as if he were about to nod off, but she'd discovered his chronic lethargy was more pose than reality.

She perched next to him on the edge of the sofa. "Have you seen Dixon?"

His mustache twitched. "Thought you weren't speaking to him."

"We had a disagreement." She spoke stiffly. "Have you seen him?"

"He left for Baker City about an hour ago. Said he wanted to contact that cop friend of his."

She bridled. "He just left me here unprotected? What kind of bodyguard is he, anyway?"

Kurt lifted an eyebrow. "He did ask me to keep an eye on you. Said he thinks you'll be safe as long as you don't leave the lodge."

"He thinks that, does he?"

Kurt didn't comment.

In the silence she could hear the snapping of the flames, the ticking of the mantel clock. It was hard to hang on to her anger in such a peaceful setting.

Kurt stretched like a big cat. "Want to play a game of Scrabble?"

In the end, four of them played. Ginger and one of the regular guests, Mitzi Murtaugh, a retired college professor from LaGrande, joined Kurt and Alex in a cut-throat competition.

Ginger had just played *qiviut* on the triple-word score when someone rang the doorbell.

"Challenge!" shouted Mitzi, reaching for the dictionary. "There's no such word. I'm onto you, Ginger. Remember the time you tried to slip *yummox* past me?"

Ginger gave her a superior smile. "I wasn't trying to slip anything past you, Mitzi. I was confusing it with *lummox*. Qiviut is a real word. Honest. It's the wool of the undercoat of the musk ox."

The bell rang again. "I'll get it." Kurt, who was wrapped around his chair like a pretzel, slowly untwisted himself and sauntered to the door.

"Damn!" Mitzi slammed the book shut. "He's right."

"Told you so." Ginger's grin was unbearably smug.

Kurt swung the big front door open as the bell rang a third time. An Oregon State Police officer filled the doorway.

"Is there an Alexandra Roundtree staying here?"

Something was very wrong. She knew it. Alex stood up so abruptly that she spilled her tiles across the Scrabble board. "I'm Alexandra Roundtree. What is it? What's happened?"

"Do you know a private investigator from Brunswick named Dixon Yano?"

"Sure. He's my cousin," said Kurt.

"He's working for me," Alex added. Her stomach spasmed, then tried to crawl up her esophagus. "Why? What's wrong?"

"There's been an accident. Apparently, the brakes on his Jeep failed."

Alex took a deep breath. I'm not going to faint, she told herself. "Is he all right?" He must be alive, and conscious too. Otherwise, how would the man know her name? Unless . . .

She stared at the burly patrolman in growing horror. Unless the whole thing was a lie. Unless the man was just pretending to be an Oregon State Police officer. Trust no one, Dixon had said.

Her voice shook, but didn't break. "I'd like to see some identification, please."

THIRTEEN

"No, Alexandra." Kurt slipped an arm around her shoulders. "He's on the up-and-up. I swear. Bill, put your badge away. This is Bill Umphrey, Alex. He lives down the road. Ginger and I have known him for years." He caught her gaze. "He's one of the good guys, honest."

Alex shivered. She was getting paranoid, not a good sign. She turned to the state trooper. "Where's Dixon?"

"At Saint Elizabeth's Hospital in Baker City. His injuries aren't serious," Officer Umphrey assured her quickly. "He was more worried about you than about the gash in his forehead. Made me promise to tell you what'd happened so you wouldn't spend the night worrying. They're keeping him overnight for observation."

The muscles in Alex's stomach tightened. "I thought you said he wasn't seriously injured."

"He's not." Officer Bill Umphrey had a direct gaze and a deep, reassuring voice. "Just mad as hell because the sawbones refused to release him. He asked me to tell you to sit tight."

Alex gave a short bark of laughter. "Forget that!"

"Ms. Roundtree, he's worried about you. He's afraid that without him around, you might do something stupid."

She watched his expression change to one of chagrin as he realized what he'd just said.

"Is that a direct quote or are you paraphrasing?"

Umphrey stammered. "I . . . no . . . I . . ."

Before he could finish whatever he'd been trying to say, Shelby and Mark walked in on the scene, arguing loudly, a circumstance that afforded Alex a moment of guilty pleasure.

"I waited in the ski shop for almost twenty minutes. What were you doing all that time?" Mark was in a snit. She'd always hated it when he'd used that tone on her.

"I told you already. I was in the ladies' room. I wasn't feeling well."

Shelby didn't look well. She was paler than normal despite having just spent the whole day outdoors.

Suddenly she noticed the uniformed trooper. If possible, she grew even paler, every vestige of color draining from her face. "What's happened?" she asked in a reedy voice Alex scarcely recognized. "Has there been an accident?"

Alex stepped forward. "Yes. Didn't you notice the patrol car parked outside?"

Shelby's jaw went slack. Alex thought for a second she was about to faint. "I—we parked in back and walked around."

"I didn't leave the lights on," Umphrey said. "Thought it might be bad for business."

"Bless you, dear man." Ginger jumped up. "For that

you earn a reward—a plate of my special maple sticky buns." He bustled off toward the kitchen.

Mark frowned as he struggled to follow the conversation. "You all look pretty healthy to me. If there was an accident, who was hurt?"

"Dixon," Alex said. "He's in the hospital in Baker City. Officer Umphrey assured me his injuries are minor, but I intend to judge for myself. That's where I'm headed now."

"We can drive you, can't we, Mark?" Shelby shot Mark a look of appeal.

He frowned. "But it's Christmas Eve. We'll miss dinner."

What a jerk. Alex could scarcely believe she'd ever been so misguided as to imagine herself in love with this man. "Mark's car's only a two-seater."

"I'll run you in," Kurt offered.

"You've got your hands full taking care of your other guests. I'll call a taxi."

"No need. Ginger can handle things here. I'd like to check out those 'minor injuries' firsthand anyway. Besides, Dixon deputized me, remember? He'd kill me if I let you go all that way alone." He sighed in resignation. "He's probably going to kill me anyway for letting you go at all."

Alex set her jaw. "Don't worry. I'll deal with Dixon."

Candy, the cute blonde nurse, fluffed his pillows and adjusted the bed for the second time. "There. How's that, Dixon? Better?"

"Fine." In fact, this whole hospital thing was turning out to be a lot more enjoyable than he'd expected.

"Here's your dinner." Darbie, the even cuter brunette, set his dinner tray on the bedside table. She cranked on the handle that adjusted the table's height until she was satisfied, then swung it across his legs. Whipping the plate covers off with all the flair of a professional magician, she conjured up sirloin tips, a baked potato, and asparagus with hollandaise. "If you need more sour cream . . . just press the call button." She did this cute little Scarlett O'Hara thing with her eyelashes.

"You know how to press the call button, don't you?" Alexandra glared at him from the doorway. "Just put your finger down, and push." Her scathing look lashed across the room at the two young nurses. "I noticed on the way in how well trained the other patients are. There are at least five lights lit up along this side of the hall alone."

Candy scuttled off at a trot, but Darbie was made of sterner stuff. "Remember, if you need anything, Dixon . . . anything at all . . ."

"He'll call. He'll call."

Darbie sidled out with one last flutter of her truly extraordinary lashes.

Alexandra frowned after her. "Short skirts are so unprofessional. I'm surprised the supervisor lets her get away with wearing such a scanty uniform."

"She *is* the supervisor." Dixon hid his grin. Alexandra was jealous. Which meant she still cared for him. Which, in turn, meant she'd probably forgive him sooner or later. Yes, oh yes. Despite the twelve stitches at his hairline, life was good.

"Hi, cuz." Kurt smiled apologetically over Alexandra's shoulder.

"Thanks for bringing her down, Kurt." Dixon's voice was laced with sarcasm. "She was safe at the resort. That's why I asked her to stay there."

Kurt shrugged. "Hey, I figured I was dead meat no matter what I did. And the truth is, cuz, I'm more scared of her than of you."

"As well you should be." Alexandra feinted a punch at Kurt's midsection.

He doubled up in mock pain. "See the way the woman treats me? Do you blame me for caving in?"

Dixon grunted.

"Besides, I wanted to check out your injuries for myself."

"I'll live," Dixon assured him.

Alexandra frowned. "Don't count on it."

Kurt shot her a nervous glance. "Well, if you're all right, Dix, then I guess I'll head on back."

Coward, thought Dixon.

"Thanks for the ride," Alexandra called after Kurt's retreating back, then pulled the heavy door shut behind him.

Dixon eyed her warily. "Why did you do that?"

"What? Shut the door? I thought you might prefer to chew me out privately."

He shook his head. "I don't intend to chew you out. You shouldn't have come, but I'm glad you did."

"That's good. Because the way I see it, a few stitches in your head don't relieve you of all responsibility. I hired you to guard my body, Dixon Olaf Kenichi Yano, and that's pretty hard to do when I'm thirty miles away."

Pushing his dinner tray aside, she perched on the edge of his bed. "I'm glad you're not angry with me, but it's a shame to waste all this lovely privacy." She leaned closer until her lips were within a hairsbreadth of his.

"Definitely." Smiling, Dixon closed the gap to capture her lips. Sweet, soft, and wildly intoxicating—that was Alexandra. He only hoped the nurse didn't come in to check his vitals before he had a chance to calm down. The blood pounded in his ears like heavy surf and he suspected his blood pressure was off the chart.

Alexandra was the first to pull away. She nestled against his chest with a little sigh of contentment. "I thought I'd lost you, Dixon. When that cop said you'd been in an accident . . ." She sat up, cradling his face gently between her hands. Her tender expression filled all the empty spaces in his soul. She loved him. She hadn't said it, but he knew. Her face said it for her. "I don't want to lose you, Dixon."

They were watching *Home Alone* on the TV mounted on swivel brackets in the corner. Macaulay Culkin had just unrolled his battle plan when Mark and Shelby strolled in.

Shelby plopped a stack of supermarket tabloids down on Dixon's bed. "Thought you'd want to keep up on the latest UFO abductions."

"Thanks."

Shelby smiled and passed Alexandra a large Styrofoam cup. "We didn't forget you, either, Alex. Here's some of Ginger's special eggnog. I know you missed dinner. And this stuff really is delicious. 'To die for' as Ginger so modestly puts it."

"Sounds wonderful. Thanks, Shelby." Alexandra set the cup on Dixon's table.

Catherine Mulvany
198

"Better drink up before it gets warm. Lukewarm egg-nog is disgusting." Shelby stuck out her tongue.

Alexandra didn't like eggnog, Dixon remembered, though he doubted Shelby would suspect it from the carefully polite expression on her cousin's face. Time to change the subject. "Surely you two didn't drive all the way to Baker City just to bring us gifts."

Shelby laughed. "No, we're playing hooky—going to a movie. The entertainment at the Last Resort leaves a little to be desired. When we left, they were playing charades." She rolled her eyes.

"I suggested Sun Valley." Mark Jordan looked and sounded like a petulant child.

"They're always so crowded over Christmas." Shelby turned to Dixon. "How are you doing? We were sorry to hear about your accident. The roads are terrible, aren't they? Mark and I saw two cars stranded in the ditch on our way down this evening."

As Shelby spoke she drifted about the room, settling finally on the empty bed.

"Actually, my accident was no accident." Dixon's little bombshell galvanized the others.

"What?" Jordan and Alexandra demanded in a surprised duet.

"How do you know?" Shelby asked.

"I didn't slide off the road by chance. My brakes went out as I came down the grade."

"Brakes do wear out." Jordan talked as if he'd just been hired to represent the brake manufacturer.

"I had a brake job last month. This was no accident. Someone drained my brake fluid."

"How frightening!" Shelby shuddered.

Jordan placed his hand on Alexandra's. "Can we

talk?" he asked softly, so softly Dixon couldn't actually hear the words. Luckily, he counted lipreading among his talents.

"Alexandra has nothing to say to you, Jordan."

"I can speak for myself, thank you." She shot him a dirty look. "Let's take a walk," she said to Mark.

The look on Shelby's face as they left the room would have withered a lesser woman.

Dixon clicked the TV off just as the tarantula landed on Daniel Stern's chest.

"I hate that kid," Shelby remarked.

Dixon figured she was referring to Macaulay Culkin, since the closest flesh-and-blood kids were over in pediatrics.

Shelby moved across to the bedside chair Alexandra had just vacated. She nudged the cup with her finger. "It's going to go bad if she doesn't drink it."

"What does Jordan want to talk to Alexandra about?"

Shelby clenched her hands together tightly. She spoke without looking up. "He loves her."

"Bull!" Dixon felt like breaking something—preferably Jordan's face. "He loves her money."

Shelby gave a sad little smile. "Same thing."

Dixon swore. "She's too good for him." He looked hard at the redhead. "And so are you."

She shrugged. "You can't pick who you're going to fall for. It doesn't work that way." She fell silent, staring again in seeming fascination at her long scarlet nails, picking nervously at the chipped edge on her right thumbnail.

"You're a nice guy, Dixon," she said at length. "I really am sorry about your accident." She rubbed her broken nail across the leather of her handbag. "It's a shame when innocent people have to suffer." She glanced up. "Did you hear about the poor old homeless man who died in the fire at Gemini Gifts? Talk about bad luck."

Dixon's smile was grim. "I don't believe in luck—just fate."

"I love you, Alex. I know how it looks, my coming up here with Shelby, but the truth is our relationship is strictly platonic."

"Save your breath, Mark. I'm not buying this."

"Alex." He closed his eyes, massaging his forehead as if he had a headache.

Alex suspected the headache was fiction, the gesture a delaying tactic. He was probably racking his brain for a fresh approach.

"Alex, I . . ." Gazing soulfully into her eyes, Mark gripped her hands. "Darling, you've got to believe me. I love you so much. I don't think I can live without you."

She smiled. "At least not in the manner to which you'd like to become accustomed. No showcase home in the Loomises' oh-so-exclusive neighborhood. No Porsche in the garage." She sighed in exaggerated sympathy.

His grip on her fingers tightened painfully. He glanced quickly over his shoulder down the length of the deserted hall. "I won't take no for an answer." He jerked her into his arms, then ground his mouth against hers. The punishing travesty of a kiss left her lower lip throbbing.

"Let me go, Mark!" She tried to twist free, but his

grip was like iron. "This isn't like you. What have you been doing? Taking lessons from your boss?"

"I need you, Alex." He gave her earlobe a painful nip. "God, baby, I'm hot for you. Feel." Mark seized her hand and pressed it to his crotch.

Alex struggled, trying to pull her hand away, but he held it fast. "You're disgusting."

"You know you want it, Alex. You want it just as much as I do." He rolled his pelvis, pressing himself against her hand.

"All I want, Mark, is to see the last of you. Dixon was right. You are scum." Cupping the bulge beneath her fingers, she gave it a vicious twist.

His grip went slack. His eyes grew large. He doubled up, sucking in a long, ragged breath. "You bitch." His voice followed her, echoing eerily down the deserted hall. "I'll get you for this."

Shelby glanced up as Alexandra returned to Dixon's room. "Where's Mark?"

"Call the cops, Dixon." Alexandra's voice was as cold as the snow capping the Elkhorns.

"What's the problem?" Shelby asked.

"I'm charging Mark with assault. I think he's the one, Dixon, the one who's been trying to kill me. He threatened me just now. I want him behind bars."

"No!" Shelby's eyes widened in shock. Her hands flew up to cover her mouth.

Dixon reached for the phone.

"No," Shelby said again. She stood, drawing a lethal-looking .357 from her purse to emphasize her objection.

"That's my gun!"

Shelby ignored her cousin's outraged comment. "Over there, Alex." With a wave of the gun she motioned for Alexandra to step around to the far side of the bed.

Alexandra, her gaze glued to the barrel, followed Shelby's orders. "This is crazy. He's not worth it, Shelby."

"All I ever wanted was for Mark to love me. If it hadn't been for you, he would have."

"Put the gun down, Shelby." Dixon spoke calmly, trying to defuse the situation. Beneath the sheet, he kept his finger pressed to the call button.

"Don't interfere, Dixon, or I'll take you out too. I swear to God I will." Sweat beaded Shelby's pale forehead. "I know how to use this thing. Uncle Stuart taught all of us girls how to defend ourselves, remember, Alex?"

"Who taught you how to tamper with brakes?" Dixon asked.

Shelby's narrowed eyes glittered. "An old friend. Alex knows him. Danny Hall. He turned his back the day I sneaked into the Stockton Building too."

"The cops are onto you, Shelby. They paid a visit to Hall yesterday. He ratted you out."

She laughed. "Nice try, Dixon. Only I talked to Danny this morning. The cops spooked him, all right, but he'd sooner slit his own throat than give them the time of day. He's lying low until things blow over."

"Bill Umphrey stopped by just before Alexandra got here. He found a pool of brake fluid in Kurt's garage. I bet if he looks, he'll find a chip of red nail polish, too. That's how you damaged your manicure, huh?"

"I'm sorry you were hurt. Alex was the primary target."

"But when did you do it? That's what I don't understand. Are you and Jordan working together?"

"No. He has no idea what's going on. This morning I slipped away from the slopes, drove back, and played with the brakes on the Jeep. The whole operation took under half an hour and Mark never suspected a thing."

"But how did you know where to find us?" Alex asked. Dixon was glad to see she was beginning to regain her equilibrium. When she'd first realized Shelby was behind the murder attempts, she had looked shell-shocked.

"When you called Mark from old Mrs. Yano's house, her name showed up on caller ID. Using that information, I traced you."

"It was you on the snowmobile?" Alexandra looked sick.

"Right. I figured you'd bolt. Got my car and waited to see which way you ran. I followed you to the Last Resort, then drove back to Brunswick, where I convinced Mark we ought to change our plans, try Anthony Lakes for a change. He never suspected a thing."

"You were responsible for the fire at Gemini Gifts too." It was a statement, not a question. Alexandra's face was stiff with accusation.

"You have insurance." She frowned at Alexandra. "Why didn't you just drink up your eggnog like a good girl? You would have saved us all a lot of trouble."

"I don't like eggnog."

Shelby's manic laughter sent chills down Dixon's spine. "Figures."

"What's in it?" he asked. "Rat poison?"

Shelby ignored him. "I swear, Alex, you must have

more lives than a cat." She steadied the gun with both hands, aiming straight at Alexandra's chest. "Unfortunately, you're down to the last one."

"Don't do anything foolish, Shelby. You'll never get away with it." Dixon hooked the tray table with one foot and shoved it toward her, hoping to catch her off guard.

She jumped aside and leveled the gun at him. A muscle twitched under her eye. Specks of spittle appeared at the corners of her mouth. "Nobody's caught onto me yet. Not the cops. Not even Mark."

"Nobody? How about Myron?"

That's it, Alexandra. Keep her talking.

Shelby sneered. "Snoopy old bastard. Small loss to the human race he was."

Dixon stared hard at Shelby. "That's where you slipped up."

"You're wrong. No one saw a thing. They'll never be able to pin his murder on me."

Dixon shook his head. "It's too late, Shelby. You already incriminated yourself."

"Yes, but neither one of you is going to be in any condition to tell anyone anything."

Dixon kept a wary eye on the .357. "It would be senseless to kill us now. The cops already know you're guilty."

"You're lying." Tightening her grip on the gun, Shelby glanced around with a hunted expression. "How could they know?"

"Earlier you said what a shame it was about poor old Myron's body being found in the rubble of the fire. But the police never released that information to the press.

The only way you could have known about it was if you were the one who'd killed him."

"You're very sharp, Dixon Yano, private investigator." Shelby's smile did little to allay his fears. "Too bad you won't have time to tell anyone else what you figured out."

Dixon smiled. "Oh, but I already have."

Shelby's face went blank.

"When you went to the bathroom a while ago, I contacted the cops. They should be here any minute now. It's over, Shelby."

Spots of color highlighted her cheekbones like poorly applied blush. Her hands shook. The gun wobbled dangerously back and forth from Alexandra to Dixon, then back to Alexandra. "It's over when *I* say it's over." She ground the words out from between clenched teeth.

Suddenly the door swung open. Mark Jordan barged in with a scrawny hospital security guard in tow.

"There she is," Mark said. "There's the woman who assaulted me." Too absorbed in himself to notice Shelby or her gun, he pointed toward Alexandra. "I'm going to sue your butt, Alex, and before I'm done, I'll have every cent of that trust fund in my pocket. You should know better than to screw with a lawyer."

"Yes, obviously I should." Alexandra giggled hysterically.

"Get out of here, Mark." Shelby waved the gun at him.

The security guard paled, then swallowed noisily, his Adam's apple bobbing. "Do what the lady says, mister."

A series of emotions passed across Jordan's face: surprise, confusion, disbelief, anger, amusement. "What is this? A joke?"

"No joke," Dixon told him. "Shelby's the one who's been trying to kill Alexandra."

Jordan's face registered shock. "Shelby?"

"Get out, Mark. And take the guard with you. I've got some business to take care of."

Alexandra went very still. She shot Dixon a look of entreaty.

"Diversion," he mouthed. Shelby had all her attention trained on the two men backing out of the room.

"Geronimo!" Alexandra yelled at the top of her lungs, then dove under the bed to tackle Shelby's legs.

Dixon made a grab for the gun.

Shelby pulled the trigger, but she was off balance, unable to take careful aim. The bullet exploded harmlessly, though the blast itself was deafening in such close quarters.

Dixon made a second grab for the gun, successful this time, as Shelby went down under the weight of Alexandra's tackle. The redhead slammed her head against a rolling metal cabinet on the way down and went out like a light. The stainless-steel bedpan that had been perched atop the cabinet set up a metallic clangor as it bounced across the tile floor.

Darbie, the cute little nursing supervisor, shouldered her way past Mark Jordan and the security guard, a stern expression on her face. "I'm sorry," she announced, "but you'll have to leave. Visiting hours are over."

"Geronimo?" Dixon raised an eyebrow.

Alex grinned. "It was all I could think of. What took those cops so long, anyway?"

Dixon looked sheepish. "That was a bluff. I did try to

call when Shelby was in the john, but I couldn't get through." He shoved his feet into his boots.

They were alone now in Dixon's hospital room. The police had taken Shelby into custody. She had not gone quietly.

As for Mark, he'd disappeared even before the police had shown up. A coward to the end.

"What did I ever see in him?" she wondered aloud.

"Jordan?"

She nodded.

"Beats the hell out of me." Dixon eased the off-white cotton sweater over his head, careful to hold the fabric away from his stitches.

Alex tipped her head to one side, puzzling it out. "Initially, of course, his looks attracted me. Mark really is gorgeous." She sighed. "My mistake was in believing his character matched his face."

Dixon shrugged into his leather jacket and stuffed his wallet into his hip pocket. "Ready?"

"I can't believe the doctor released you after all the ruckus tonight."

Dixon grinned crookedly. "He didn't. I'm going AWOL."

"What about your head?"

"What about it? Look at my eyes, Alexandra. My pupils look fine, right?"

She nodded.

"So no concussion, which, in turn, means no need to stay."

"But where are we going?"

He pulled her into a tight embrace. "Anywhere you want. The danger's over."

"But your Jeep . . . we don't have a car."

"I called a cab."

It was over. She could scarcely believe it. Alex glanced up at Dixon's face. He was handsome, as handsome in his own way as Mark Jordan, but Dixon's face held character too. And determination. No strings, she reminded herself. Now that no one was trying to kill her, she had no more need for a bodyguard. She reached up to touch his cheek, loving the rugged line of his jaw, the raspy feel of his stubbly skin. A deep melancholy settled over her. No more danger. No more bodyguard. No more Dixon.

Dixon tilted her chin up with the gentle pressure of one finger. "Hey, cheer up! You look like you just lost your best friend." He dropped a quick kiss on her lips. "Shall we go back to the Sunridge Inn or would you prefer the Last Resort? Tell you what, if Kurt still has the dormer room free, let's take it. I can think of a few interesting uses for that Jacuzzi."

"Sure," she said. *Enjoy it while it lasts*, the pragmatist in her advised.

But I want it to last forever, the romantic argued.

Alex fell asleep on the ride back to the lodge, her head on Dixon's shoulder, his arm holding her warm and secure against his side. She didn't wake up until Dixon laid her down on the fluffy down-filled comforter that covered the king-size brass bed in the dormer room.

"What do you think?" Dixon spread his hands to indicate their surroundings. "A step up from the garage apartment, huh?"

It was indeed. Country extravagance best described the decor. Alex wondered who had chosen the lace-edged sheets, the antique armoire, the double Irish chain quilt that hung on the wall at the head of the bed. "It's gorgeous."

"Kurt did all the decorating himself," Dixon said in answer to her unspoken question. "Maybe we ought to turn him loose on our house."

"Our house?" Alex's throat felt tight. What was he talking about? Was this his not-so-subtle way of asking her to move in with him? "What about the ground rules? What about 'no strings'?"

Dixon lay down beside her. He gathered her into his arms and solemnly kissed the hollow at the base of her throat. "I love you, Alexandra. Strings don't bind any tighter than that."

Her mind whirled. "I love you, too, but what about the ground rules?"

"Ground rules be damned. You were right. I was an idiot. Mind if we dispense with this?" He tossed her sweater onto the floor and proceeded to kiss his way down her breastbone.

"But buying a house together? That sounds serious." Permanent, she wanted to say, but held her tongue for fear of scaring him off.

"My apartment's okay," he murmured between kisses, "but we'll need more room when the kids put in an appearance."

"What?" Alex struggled to a sitting position, too shocked to say anything else.

"Good idea." Dixon flicked the back clasp of her bra and drew the straps down her arms. He took one pink nipple into his mouth.

Alex fought to maintain her concentration, a difficult

task with Dixon around. His mouth on her breast was enough to drive her crazy, but when he slid one hand up her thigh, the maneuver sent little flickers of desire zapping through her abdomen. "What kids?" she managed at last.

"Ours, of course." Dixon transferred his attention to her other nipple.

"Ours?" she echoed weakly.

"Only if you're agreeable, of course. I wouldn't want to force anything on you."

"Like children?"

"Right. Remember that second condition you wouldn't let me explain?"

"I remember." Why had she ever thought his eyes sad?

"The second condition was that in the event we fell irrevocably in love with one another—" He paused. "You are irrevocably in love with me, aren't you, sweetheart?" He paused again, this time to kiss her.

His lips were warm and insistent. Say yes, they seemed to say. Say yes. "Yes," she whispered against his mouth.

"Good," said Dixon, "because I am irrevocably in love with you too. Which, as it happens, automatically renders the first condition null and void." He slid a ring on her finger. "I bought this in Baker City the other day when you were replenishing your wardrobe. I thought your finger looked a little bare. You *are* planning to make an honest man of me, aren't you?"

A smile spread across her face. Forever. The word was a song in her heart.

"Aren't you?" he prompted, nibbling at her earlobe.

"Absolutely." She gasped as his hand slid between her legs.

"Alexandra?" Dixon's whisper sent a shiver down her spine.

"What?"

"Merry Christmas."

THE EDITORS' CORNER

The new year is once again upon us, and we're ushering it in with four new LOVESWEPTs to grace your bookshelves. From the mountains of Kentucky and Nevada to the beaches of Florida, we'll take you to places only your heart can go! So curl up in a comfy chair and hide out from the rest of the world while you plan a christening party with Peggy, catch a killer with Ruth, rescue a pirate with Cynthia, and camp out in the Sierras with Jill.

First is **ANGELS ON ZEBRAS,** LOVESWEPT #866, by the well-loved Peggy Webb. Attorney Joseph Patrick Beauregard refuses to allow Maxie Corban to include zebras at their godson's christening party. Inappropriate, he says. And that's just the beginning! Joe likes his orderly life just fine, and Maxie can't help but try to shake it up by playing the brazen hussy to Joe's conservative legal eagle. Suffice it to say, a steamy yet tenuous relationship ensues, as they learn they can't keep their hands off each other! You may remember Joe and Maxie's relatives as B. J. Corban and Crash Beauregard from BRINGING UP BAXTER, LOVESWEPT #847. Peggy Webb stuns us with another sensual tale of love and laughter in this enchanting mix of sizzle and whimsy.

Ex-cop Rafe Ramirez has no choice but to become the hero of a little girl determined to save her mom in Ruth Owen's **SOMEONE TO WATCH OVER ME**, LOVESWEPT #867. TV anchorwoman Tory Chandler has been receiving dangerous riddles and rhymes written in bloodred ink. Knowing her past is about to rear its ugly head, she wants nothing more than to ignore the threats that have her on edge. Rafe can't ignore them, however, since he's given Tory's daughter his word. Protecting the beautiful temptress who so openly betrayed him is the hardest assignment he's ever had to face. Now that he's back on the road to recovery, can this compassionate warrior keep Tory safe from her worst nightmares? LOVESWEPT favorite Ruth Owen explores the healing of two wounded souls in this story of dark emotions and desperate yearnings.

In **YOUR PLACE OR MINE?**, LOVESWEPT #868, by Cynthia Powell, Captain Diego Swift wakes to find himself stranded in a time much different from his own, and becomes engaged in an argument with the demure she-devil who has besieged his home. Catalina Steadwell had prayed for help from above, though admittedly this half-drowned, naked sailor was not what she was expecting. Though Cat doesn't believe this man's ravings about the nineteenth century, she does need a man around her dilapidated house, and hires Diego as her handyman. After all, the job market for pirates has pretty much dwindled to nothing. When Diego becomes involved in a local gang war, he learns to make use of his second chance at life and love. Here's a positively scrumptious tale by Cynthia Powell that's sure to fulfill every woman's dream of a seafaring, swashbuckling hero!

In **SHOW ME THE WAY**, LOVESWEPT #869, by Jill Shalvis, Katherine Wilson ventures into the wilds of the high Sierras in a desperate attempt to stay alive. Outfitter Kyle Spencer challenges the pretty prosecutor to accompany his group in conquering the elements, but Katy is a city girl at heart. As danger stalks them through God's country, suddenly nothing in the woods is as innocent as it seems. Kyle knows that something is terrifying Katy and wants desperately to help her, but how can he when the woman won't let him near her? Their attraction grows as their time together ebbs, and soon Katy will have to make a choice. Will she entrust Kyle with her life and her heart, or will the maniac who's after her succeed in destroying her? In this journey of survival and discovery, Jill Shalvis shows us once again how believing in love can save you from yourself.

Happy reading!

With warmest wishes,

Susann Brailey

Joy Abella

Susann Brailey
Senior Editor

Joy Abella
Administrative Editor